THE MEADE LAKE SERIES

STONES
unturned

T.D. COLBERT

Stones Unturned

The Meade Lake Series, Book Two

Copyright © 2020 T.D. Colbert

Published: T.D. Colbert 2020

www.taylordanaecolbert.com

Cover Design: T.D. Colbert

Editing: Jenn Lockwood Editing

ISBN: **eBook- 978-1-7352169-3-5**

Paperback - 978-1-7352169-2-8

To you, Will. My real-life Derrick, the calm to my crazy, the bright spot in my days, the headshake to my every trip and fall. I love you.

1

I'm sitting in my car outside of Richie's Tavern, staring at the badge in my hand. It has a photo of me with my absolute best professional smile. Next to it, reads: Kaylee Jennings. And underneath my name, in big bold letters: SALES MANAGER.

Manager. I have a team of direct reports—many of whom are old enough to be my parents—after just two years of work experience post-college. How? Oh, yeah.

Because my dad is the CEO of one of Georgia's biggest tech companies. And he's been priming me to take over since I was fifteen.

When I decided I wanted to go to Clemson and told my parents I wanted to get my journalism degree, my dad chuckled.

"Kid, trust me. Go for the business degree. Maybe eventually an MBA—but you can go for that after you have a job at the company," he had told me. "That way, the company can pay for it," he had added with a wink. "Keep writing. It's a good...er...hobby."

And that's how I landed here, just two years into my

professional career, with college barely still in the rearview mirror. And on Monday morning, I start in my new role. And I'll be in that role for six months to a year. Once I've "proven myself"—which is code for "once it looks like you've been in the position long enough"—I'll get my other promotion. The big one.

Part owner.

Things have been rocky for the company over the last few years. My dad and his lawyers did some research. Turns out, women-owned businesses are sought-after, especially when it comes to federal contracts. *Women-owned.* And what better woman to "own" his company than one who shares his last name?

I sigh and chuck the badge into my bag. I fluff out my long blonde locks fried to the max by my straightener this morning. I was trying to go for the polished, professional look. You know, since I became a boss today. And not on my own merit.

I unbutton a few buttons on my blouse and tug it out from my high-waisted skirt. I take a deep breath, get out, and head inside.

The air inside of Richie's is thick with body heat and the stench of several different types of alcohol. It smells like...home.

"Well, if it isn't Miss CEO," Charlotte says to me as I make my way through the usual Friday crowd. I roll my eyes as I walk in the direction of her and Emma.

"Manager," I correct her. "And don't even start. I'll take a beer, please," I order. I slide my blazer off and pull a stool up to the table they're sitting at.

"So, how did everyone take it?" Charlotte asks, scooting closer to me. I sigh and shake my head.

"Pretty much like you'd expect," I say. "Pretty much

how anyone would react when the boss's undeserving kid gets a shoo-in job at daddy's company after they've all been working since before I was born. The only person who congratulated me was Franklin, but I know that's just because we're friends. He can't possibly think I actually deserve it."

Charlotte nods.

"Can't you refuse the promotion?" she asks. I shake my head.

"I tried that. I told him I needed a few more years. He told me that I'd be letting the company down. Our clients expect 'Jennings blood' to be present. Plus, I can't just go from sales associate to partial owner."

"Well, listen," she says, grabbing my beer from the bartender and sliding it across the table to me, "you may have gotten the job because of who you are, but you are not undeserving. You work your ass off in literally every-thing you do. You're going to kick this position's ass, too."

I smile at her as I take a big swig, letting the golden liquid slide down my throat, hoping it drowns out this feeling that's settled in my stomach since this morning.

Charlotte is a world-class, A-plus best friend. She's been by my side since first grade in Mrs. Carlisle's class. From scolding playground bullies, to facilitating my first kiss with Brennan Stern in eighth grade, to threatening my college boyfriend when he dumped me three weeks before graduation, she's been through it all with me. Her long brown waves hang over one shoulder, and I'm always thrown by how effortlessly beautiful she really is.

"Yeah, but, I mean, I'd feel the same way if I were those people, ya know? Some kid, basically, comes in and snatches it all out from under them? Yikes," Emma says, throwing back her vodka shot. I firmly stick my beer bottle down on the table between us as I glare at her. Emma has been friends with us since middle school. Our parents run in the same circles, swimming in money and thrusting us into private schools. Charlotte went to the same schools, but that was because her mom taught at our elementary school, and she got scholarships to middle and high school.

Emma and I were raised much the same, and yet, I'm always reminded at how vastly different we turned out. She embraces the "Bad and Boujee" lifestyle. She doesn't let anything touch her skin unless it's designer, and she—much like myself—hasn't struggled for much. The big difference between us is that I work. Hard. Classes, running, college. Anything that I take on, I work at. Emma...doesn't. And so far, her parents' money has made it so that no work is no obstacle.

I'm nursing the same beer an hour later, glaring at Charlotte from across the bar. She's happily batting her eyelashes and seductively chewing on the rim of her glass. The guy she's been talking to all night looks like he just walked off of a professional baseball field and into Richie's Tavern. He's completely jacked with a little bit of scruff looking like it was blown onto his face by some sort of angel. His dark hair is tousled in that model-type way, and he is turning on the charm tonight.

Emma is giving her best half-ass laugh to one of his less attractive friend's jokes, and I'm just...here. Alone. Again.

I know I'm not one of the girls that makes you stop and say *whoa*. I get it. But I've always thought of myself as, like, a high six, maybe a seven. It's not that I don't get hit on when we go out. I do. It's that I am just unimpressed by the slim pickings of the Georgia, early-twenties dating scene. We grew up in Lenburn, a teeny-tiny town on the outskirts of Atlanta. Charlotte lives in the next town over, and Emma lives downtown with a few roommates in an apartment her parents are definitely footing the bill for. Me? An apartment across town that I have no business living in on my salary. Except that I, uh, don't pay for it all myself. But it's less than two miles from my parents, so Dad said it was "perfect" and offered a monthly—an open-ended—stipend. People ask us why we never moved into the city. My dad says it's the taxes. I think it's because my dad can look like a king here in Lenburn. Big fish in a small pond sort of deal.

We bounce back and forth between downtown and here depending on the weekend. Charlotte and Emma seem to find the fun wherever we land. But not me. The whole picking someone out on a phone screen and then summoning them to you with the sole intent of getting in their pants has lost its appeal to me.

I like to think I'm too intellectual, or maybe it's because I feel like the bedroom antics of today's men aren't up to the standards of the romance novels Charlotte is always thrusting at me. Either way, I'm sort of thinking alone is the way to go. At least for a little while.

"Kay? Hello? You good?" Emma asks, coming over to the bar to order another round for her and tonight's catch.

"Uh, yeah, I'm good. How is tonight's company?" I ask sarcastically. She rolls her eyes as she picks up the glasses.

"Well, you would know if you hadn't told their friend you had an incurable eye-goop disease," she says, pursing her lips out at me. I can't help but laugh. I've been watching one of the guys in their group sneak stares at me all night since, trying to figure out which eye it is.

Sometimes I just have too much fun with these jokers.

"I'm gonna take these back over there. Are you sure you don't want to just come sit?" she asks. I smile and shake my head.

"I'm good."

Emma pauses for a minute then turns back to me.

"Ya know, Kay, I'm not saying this to be hurtful, but I just don't know why you even come with us anymore. You barely drink, and you're not into anyone who seems remotely interested in you. I guess I just...I hope you figure out what you're looking for. Watching you sit alone all these nights makes me kinda sad," she says. Before I can respond, she turns back around and walks back to the table she and Charlotte and their gentleman callers are sitting at. I see Charlotte lift her eyes to me, and I feel shame.

Emma is my best friend.

But Charlotte...she's a soulmate.

She's one of those people who knows how I'm feeling, what I'm thinking, how I'll react to something before I even know myself. She can read me from across the room, and she makes her way to me.

"What did she say?" she asks. I smile. Charlotte is an angel.

She's a nurse at Atlanta's Children's Hospital, and they are so damn lucky to have her.

"Nothin'," I say with a smile. She puts her hand on her hip and shoots me a look. "It's not important. Really. How is Mr. Hotstuff back there?"

She smiles, turning back to him then back to me.

"He's...actually really cool. He's been in the minors for a few years," she says. I smile and nod. He *is* a baseball player.

"That's cool," I say.

"Don't look now," she says, stepping in closer to me, "but dude in the black shirt at the back...he's been eyeing you up for the last half hour."

My head perks up, and my eyes start scanning the room because as soon as someone says, "Don't look," we, as humans, can't help but do the exact opposite.

I see a group of guys in the back corner, but none of them seem particularly interested in me.

I see a group of women chatting and laughing too loud, and I see their eyes all floating across to the back of the room.

And then I see the guy.

He has about five pairs of eyes on him, but his are on me.

When our eyes meet, he doesn't shy away. He stares into mine with a fierceness that makes me a little unstable.

"See," Charlotte whispers.

And then the guy stands.

He's tall with shoulders that stretch out his shirt. His forearms are toned and hard-looking, and I can see the ripples of his chest underneath the fabric.

"I think he's coming over here," Charlotte whispers. "You should talk to him."

Lately, I'd literally do anything in my power to avoid a situation like this. But right now, I can't move. I don't want to. I don't want to take my eyes off of him. Nah, no avoiding this today. I'm taking this one head-on. I keep my eyes on his and reach over for Charlotte's glass in her hand. I throw back whatever's left in it then squint my eyes at the bitterness of whatever the fuck that was. I hand it back to her, wipe my lip, and make a beeline right for him.

Then, he starts walking toward me. This is a small bar, but right now, the distance between us feels huge. I want to close in on it, close in on him.

Finally, we're within a few feet of each other. I smile at him, but his eyes are wide, like he's...in shock? Surprised? Maybe I looked different from across the room.

Suddenly, I'm self-conscious. I fluff my hair a bit, pulling it down off my shoulder. I cross an arm over my body.

"H-hi—"

"Are you Kaylee?" he asks before I can get a full word out. My eyebrows knit together, and I cock my head. "Kaylee Jennings?"

When I started kindergarten that following year, I didn't mention her. I said I was an only child. I told everyone I had no siblings, just like Mama had told me to do.

But now, almost twenty years later, this devilishly handsome man appears and seems to know about her? Seems to know more about me than I do?

He's looking at me, and I can see the want in his eyes. The hope. And even through this enormous wave of uncertainty he's brought on me, I feel a little at ease when I look at him.

"If you want, you can just follow me in your car," he says. "I don't want to make you uncomfortable. I just want you to come."

I can see in his eyes how badly he wants me to say yes. Only, I can't figure out what's in it for him. Why would May not want me to come?

Why the *fuck* have I been told she's been dead for almost twenty years?

"I should call my mom—" I start to say, but his face immediately furrows into a frown.

"Okay," he says, "but you should know that she is going to tell you not to come."

There's something about the confidence in what he's saying, something about the certainty, that I know it's true. I know he's right. I just don't know why.

"Can I just...I just need to talk to my friend real quick," I say, putting a hand to my head. He nods and scoots back, holding a hand out toward the door.

"Of course. I'll wait for you out here," he says. I nod and slink back inside.

Charlotte and Emma rush me as I walk through the door.

"What happened?" Charlotte asks, lifting my arms like she's checking for some sort of hidden injury or something. "Did he say something?"

"Did he hurt you?" Emma asks, and my eyes zip to her.

"You could see us the whole time," I say. "You know he didn't lay a hand on me."

"Well...what did he say?" Charlotte asks.

"He wants me to go on a road trip with him," I blurt out. Their eyes become saucers. And then Emma laughs.

"Right," she says between giggles. But she stops abruptly when she realizes I'm serious. "Wait...what?"

"He knows...a relative of mine. That lives up in Maryland. Some little lake town," I say. "He showed me a photo and everything. It's definitely her."

"I don't understand. What relative? Why didn't this relative come down?" Charlotte asks. These are all good questions, and ones that I'm not so sure I really understand the answers to.

"Wait a second...you're not thinking of actually going, are you?" Emma asks. There's something in her voice, something in her tone, that doesn't feel as...concerned as Charlotte. It's more accusatory.

"I...I haven't decided," I say.

"Kaylee, you've got to be kidding," she says, crossing her arms over her BCBG blouse. "You just met him. Do you even know his last name? And besides, can you imagine the conniption your parents would have?"

I lift my eyes to her again.

"I know, they'd freak out. I don't even know him, and he's—"

She takes a few steps closer to me.

"Exactly," she says, almost in a whisper. "It's one thing for you to run off with a guy you barely know. But if your dad found out he was... Can you imagine?"

I take a step back from her, my eyes trained on hers. Then I look out the window at Derrick.

I didn't even realize he was black.

I saw his eyes. I saw his arms, his smile. I heard the words he spoke. I saw the fondness in his eyes when he talked about my grandmother.

In this moment, while some massive family secret has just been revealed, and I'm on the verge of making a pretty risky decision, my thoughts are all on my friend. And how we were raised similarly, and yet, turned out so different. And my heart breaks a little, because I know that we can't come back fully from this. She's just confirmed another major difference between us.

"If my dad found out he was *what*, Emma?" I ask her. I want her to say it. Out loud. She stumbles backward, blinking wildly. Charlotte clears her throat, trying to get rid of some of the awkwardness.

"Oh, I don't mean— I mean, you know *I* don't care, I just...you know how your dad is. How *both* of our dads are. I mean, they would never say it, but—"

"But *you* did, Emma," I say.

I turn on my heel and walk out the front door of Richie's. Derrick pops off the wall, his eyebrows raised.

"Kay," I hear Charlotte say. I pause and turn back to her slowly. She walks toward me and lifts my hand into hers. Then she pulls me into a long, warm hug. "Please be careful." She lets me go and walks toward Derrick. She sticks her hand out.

"I'm Charlotte," she says. He nods and takes her hand.

"Derrick. It's nice to meet you," he says. She smiles.

"I'm her best friend. I need your license, please."

He looks at her, perplexed, then looks to me. I just shrug. He pulls it out of his wallet and hands it to her. She snaps a picture of it on her phone.

"Just in case I need to come find you." He smiles and nods.

"That's my car, too, if you want to snap a picture of it," he tells her. She smiles back.

"Ya know, in seventeen years of being her best friend, never have I ever been left out of something. I know all of her secrets. So, if she's keeping yours, consider yourself lucky."

He nods nervously, and I swallow.

Because I don't think he's keeping his own secrets.

I think he's keeping mine.

3

Luckily, I have a bag in my car packed for what was supposed to be a stay at Charlotte's apartment, but what has now turned into me taking a ten-hour road trip to figure out why everyone in my life has lied to me since I was five. No big deal.

"Do you need anything else?" he asks. I think for a minute about driving back to my parents' house, storming through the door with the picture of May, and demanding answers.

But something tells me that, after twenty years of keeping secrets, they probably won't be too eager to tell them right now. So, instead, I'll do the more prudent thing and follow this handsome stranger to God-knows-where in search of answers that they won't give me.

"Nah," I tell him. "You have washers and dryers up in Meade Lake, right?" I ask him, holding my bag in the air. He smiles and nods.

"Nah, we just wash everything in the lake," he says with a shrug. I stare at him wide-eyed for a second before I realize he's kidding. "Okay, then, you ready to head out?"

I turn back to Richie's for a minute, looking through the window.

I nod, and we exchange phone numbers.

"We can pull off for gas and food in Charlotte," he tells me. "I'll call you, and we can find a place to stop."

"Cool," I tell him. He turns to walk to his car but pauses and turns back to me.

"Hey," he says. I look up at him. "We're gonna make it. Don't worry."

I'm thrown off by his sensitivity, his social awareness of what's going on in my head right now. I smile at him and nod.

I get in my car and reach for my duffel on the backseat. I pull out a pair of jeans and slide them on up under my skirt. I pull on a t-shirt then unbutton the rest of my blouse and slip it out from behind me. Then, I put the car in reverse and pull out behind him.

WE'VE BEEN DRIVING for about two hours, and I'm suddenly very aware of the fact that it's eleven at night, and I've been up since the crack of dawn. I didn't really think this through when I opted to drive from Georgia to Maryland.

Finally, my phone lights up.

"Hello?" I say.

"Hey," he says, and my heart does this little skip at just the sound of his voice.

"At this point, most places are going to be closed. But there's a twenty-four-hour rest stop off the next exit.

We can get gas and some snacks to hold us over, if that works for you?"

A rest stop. With a stranger. Should be totally safe.

"Sure," I say. "That's fine."

A few minutes later, we're pulling off the highway and pulling into the gas station. As I'm digging through my purse for my wallet, I hear the *thump* of my gas tank being opened and unscrewed.

"What are you doing?" I ask him.

"You're following me up the whole east coast," he says. "The least I can do is pump your gas for you."

The chivalry almost knocks me back into my seat.

"You don't have to do that," I tell him.

"I'm just glad you're here," he says with this absolute *killer* of a smile. I can't help but smile back.

"Well, I'll go grab us some snacks. It's the least I can do. What can I get you?" I ask.

He thinks for a minute.

"How about something sweet for now, and something salty for later?" he says. I smile and nod.

"You got it," I say.

I'm back out in two minutes with arms full of chips, chocolate bars, and gummy candies. He laughs when he sees me, but as he reaches out to help me, his phone rings. There's a look of concern in his eyes as he lifts them to me.

"Sorry, it's my mom," he says.

"No, please," I say, waving him off as I set everything down on the roof of my car and dig for my keys. As I'm fiddling with my key fob, I hear a scream that chills me to my bones.

I turn to see Derrick storming across the parking lot, kicking a giant dumpster at the back corner. He clasps his hands behind his head then backs up against the building, sinking slowly toward the ground.

I stand behind him, wide-eyed and wondering what the fuck I'm supposed to do next.

Then, I see him drop his head between his shoulders, and I see his shoulders start to shudder. Hesitantly, I take another step closer to him.

"Derrick?" I say.

He brings his hand to his face, swiping it down before he looks up at me slowly. He brings himself back to his feet, but he can't bring his eyes to mine.

"She's dead," he says just above a whisper.

"What?" I ask. He takes a step closer to me so we're just inches apart. I can feel my heart rate accelerating, and I don't know if it's the news of my grandmother's death, the fact that I thought she already *was* dead, or the devastatingly beautiful man in front of me who is so broken up about it.

"My mom just called. I'm so sorry, Kaylee," he says, his voice cracking and broken. "I really thought I could get you there in time. I'm so sorry."

I step toward him, and without thinking about it, I step up on my tiptoes and wrap my arms around his neck. To my misery, he smells like...I don't even know. Aftershave and...pine, maybe? Whatever it is, it's not conducive to me being consoling.

"Hey," I whisper, "it's okay. It's not your fault. You tried," I tell him, but while I say the words, it hits me how fucking weird this is. I'm standing in a gas station parking lot, hugging a stranger, consoling him over the death of *my* grandmother.

What the hell is happening?

We stand like this for a few more minutes, but then he pulls apart slowly.

"I can't believe she's gone," he says. And now that I think about it, I can't believe it, either. *After all this time…*

I don't remember a whole lot about my Gran May, but I do remember that I loved her. I remember feeling so heartbroken that she had died. I should probably feel like that now, but I don't, and I feel guilty about it.

I step apart from him after I become increasingly aware that my arms were still around him.

"Look," he says, "if you want to go back, I totally get it. But if you still want to see Meade Lake, you're welcome to follow me back. My mom mentioned, too, that you'll be getting a summons soon anyway to go over May's will."

May's will?

I think for a minute.

I came with him in the first place for answers.

Answers that I still don't have.

In fact, I think, at this juncture, now I have more questions.

"I want to come," I tell him. And if I'm not mistaken, there's a hint of a smile playing on his lips. "But I think I need to get a room for the night. I don't think I'll make it the rest of the way. Not with that news."

He nods.

"Yeah, of course," he says. "I saw signs for a hotel right down the road. Let's head that way, and we can take off early tomorrow."

I follow him another mile or so down the road to a shady-looking hotel, but at this point, I'd sleep in my damn car. We check in at the front desk, and the woman looks at him peculiarly when we tell her we need two rooms.

He sticks out his card, but I jump to yank mine from my wallet and offer it up. He holds his hand up.

"Let me, please," he says. I start to protest, but he shakes his head. "The first leg of this trip has not turned out as planned. Please, at least let me get the rooms."

I swallow and take a step back.

The woman behind the desk turns around to the keys, and when she turns back, she hands them to us with a smirk.

"They're adjoining—ya know, just in case," she says with a wink. Derrick nods slowly and thanks her, and as we turn down the hallway toward the elevator, I can't hold in my laugh any longer.

"'Just in case,'" I mock her as the doors close, and we both start laughing. His laugh is warm and hearty and makes my whole body stand at attention. I clear my throat as I think again about what she was suggesting and how, if these were any other circumstances, I would definitely not be opposed to knocking on that adjoining door.

As Derrick bends down to grab my bag for me when the doors open, I realize that I might not be completely opposed to it right now, either.

"Well, this is us," he says as we walk down the hallway a bit to rooms 304 and 305.

"Great," I say, unlocking my door and taking my bag from him. "Thank you, Derrick."

He smiles and nods.

"Goodnight," he says.

"Night," I say back.

I strip down to my underwear and my tank top,

brush my teeth in the stained sink, and slip onto the sheets after I've taken the comforter off with one finger and thrown it on the floor. I've seen those blacklight reports. No thanks.

But just as I'm settling in, I hear the sliding glass door to Derrick's balcony open. I stand back up and tug on the pair of sweatpants I had in my bag. I move toward the door that connects our rooms, but when I press my ear against it, it opens slightly. I swallow, take a breath, and make my way in. When I walk across his room, I see him, standing out on his balcony, staring out over Charlotte. And to my pleasant surprise, he doesn't have a shirt on. His rippling back muscles are tight and flexed as he hunches over the railing. The moonlight bounces off his beautifully dark skin. And although I want to drool over the sight, I can tell, just from his stance, that he's hurting. I make my way to the door and tap gently on the glass. He jumps as he turns to me.

"Hey," he says, raising an eyebrow and crossing his arms over his chest in modesty. My eyes dance across it, big and broad, the curves of his muscles putting me in some sort of trance.

"Turns out the adjoining door is just a facade," I tell him with a shrug.

"Is that so?" he asks, a smile tugging at one corner of his mouth. I nod.

"You okay?" I ask as I step up closer to him, gazing out over the city lights. He nods.

"Yeah, yeah," he says. He pauses for a moment. "I just can't believe I wasn't there."

I look up at him.

"Mama, she's heartbroken, and...everyone else. And I didn't get to say goodbye."

I take a step closer to him without even noticing it.

"I'm sorry," he says, turning to me. "I can't believe I'm sitting here whining about this to you of all people." He lifts his eyes to mine. "I know things don't make much sense right now, but I'm so sorry for your loss, Kaylee."

I swallow as I take another step closer to him. That aftershave-pine combo is kicking all of my senses into high gear, and my eyes meet his.

Slowly, I reach my hand out to his and grab hold of it.

"I thought she died twenty years ago," I say with a sad smile. "So, I'm sorry for *your* loss."

He reaches his hand out and takes my other hand.

"I know it's only been a few hours, but I can tell that May missed out on so much by not knowing you," he whispers. He looks down at our hands intertwined and quickly drops mine. I feel my heart rate kick up.

"Derrick," I say, staring into his eyes.

"Hmm?"

I clear my throat.

"Why did my parents tell me she was dead?" I whisper. He draws in a long, slow breath and drops his head. He wraps his hands around my wrists.

"I promise you, you will have answers. Tomorrow, okay?" he says. He lifts his big brown eyes to mine, and I can see he's pleading with me not to press him. So I don't. The sensation of his skin on mine is making my breath catch in my throat, and I swear he has to be able to hear my heart beating in my chest. I take a step closer to him, feeling that same heat that came over me when I first laid eyes on him at the bar. I tilt my head up to him slowly, my eyes catching his. He swallows, and I watch his Adam's apple jump. His lips are round and full, and he's got his bottom lip between his teeth as his eyes scan my face. I take one more step toward him so that our bodies are as close as possible without actually touching. He reaches a hand up slowly, cupping the side of my face. This overwhelming possession comes over me, and I want to taste him. I want his lip between *my* teeth. My palms feel clammy. No, I don't just *want* him. I *need him.* I never do this. Well, hardly ever. It's been a long time since I threw my inhibitions to the wind and just gave myself what I wanted. But since the moment I laid eyes on him yesterday, I knew I wanted him in ways I've never wanted another man. Just giving in to the animalistic desires, his body on mine, running my fingers over every curve of his muscles. My chest heaves with heavy breaths as I decide whether or not to wait for him to make the move or just do it myself. Take what I want.

But then he makes a move.

Back.

He clears his throat again nervously and takes a small step backward. His hands slide down mine until he drops them completely, and with them goes my stomach.

"I'm sorry," he whispers. I shake my head.

"Don't be sorry," I say. "You didn't have to let go." His eyes jump up to mine again, and he narrows them at me.

"Yeah, I did," he says, reaching a hand up to rub the back of his head. "Yeah, I really did."

He turns toward the skyline again. "Sorry, Kaylee. That won't happen again."

I nod slowly, letting his words sink down on me with all their weight.

"It's really okay——" I try to interject, but he shakes his head.

"It's not," he says, a firmness to his voice that wasn't there before. "It won't happen again."

I'm not sure what this line is, but he's drawn it. It's big and thick, and I have a feeling it won't be crossed. I nod again and turn toward the door.

"Goodnight, Derrick," I say. He gives me a sad smile.

"Goodnight, Kaylee."

I flop back onto my bed, heat raging through my body and settling in the pit of my stomach. He doesn't want this. He doesn't want *me*. And now I need to figure out a way to calm down my lady boner and forget that the last five minutes even happened. I turn on my side and close my eyes, trying desperately to calm myself.

But after another hour, all I can do is roll back over and stare up at the ceiling, and it has nothing to do with the lumpy hotel mattress or the fact that there's an extra-hot man lying in another bed just a few feet away.

It has more to do with the fact that my parents don't even know I'm on this quest to understand their decades-long lies. It's that I don't even know where I'm going or who I'm going to meet. It's that everyone else seems to know the deepest secrets of my life that I didn't even know I had.

And tomorrow could be the day when everything comes to light. When I step foot in Meade Lake, I plan to leave no stone unturned.

4

W e're both up and in the lobby of the hotel by seven fifteen—a half-hour before we planned to meet.

"Couldn't sleep?" he asks me, that dangerously dazzling smile hitting me like a freight train.

"Nah, too worked up, I guess," I say with a smile and shrug. He chuckles.

"Worked up in a good way or a bad way?"

I smile up at him. *Worked up because of the fire you started in me then put out before it got good.*

"A little of both, I guess," I admit. He nudges my shoulder with his as we walk to the front desk to check out.

"You got this," he says. He hands his key over, and we head out to his car.

For the rest of the drive, he calls me every hour or so. He pretends like he's just checking in to see if I need a break. But when I tell him I'm fine, we stay on, passing the time, telling stories, and even laughing. I like the sound of his voice, and each time I hear it, my stomach flutters. He gives me this sense of calm, even though I have no idea what's waiting for me on the other end of this trip.

Finally, we cross the Maryland state line, and my stomach flips again. Only, this time, it's heavy with nerves and the weight of a million questions in my gut. My palms are sweating as I grip the steering wheel. Like clockwork, my phone rings.

"Hello?" I answer.

"Hey," he says, that deep, smooth voice calming me down almost instantly. "We're almost there."

"I saw," I tell him.

"Still feelin' okay about coming?" he asks. I swallow. It's like he can read my mind.

"A little more, uh, uneasy about it now," I admit. He's silent for a moment.

"In about twenty seconds, look out your window," he tells me. There's a long silence while I wait, and then I see what he's talking about.

The sky is the most brilliant shade of indigo I've ever seen, streaked with deep pinks and magenta. The mountains around us are shades of black as the sun slides down behind them, and we make it to a bridge. As we drive over it, I look down at the lake below, deep, dark blues and greens moving beneath me. Boats drive through it, leaving trails of white in their wake.

And suddenly, I feel like I can breathe a little more.

All I feel is the beauty around me.

All I feel is calm for a moment.

"Wow," is all I can manage to say. I hear him chuckle on the other end.

"Yeah," he says. "It's gonna be okay, Kaylee."

· · ·

He leads me through the town of Meade Lake, and I see people everywhere—on the water, on boats, in shops, sitting on patios eating and drinking. We pass a big sign that reads *Willington Lake and Ski Resort*, and I see a huge parking lot filled with cars up ahead. Once we pass through town, he leads me across another small bridge, and we turn down a wooded road that reads *Wake Way*. After a few more minutes, he makes a slight left turn into a gravel driveway, and I follow close behind. We pull up to a modest wooden house with a few cars parked in front of it. I get out and stretch my legs, taking in my surroundings. Tall pines poke out from every direction, camouflaging the house. I can see the shimmer of the water through the trees behind the house, and I take in a deep gulp of mountain air. I've never breathed air like this before. Clear, uncomplicated, untouched air.

"Where are we?" I ask him.

"We're at my mom's house," he says. "This is where I grew up." I look up at the house again and smile. It would have been amazing to grow up in a place like this. "I'm sorry you won't be meeting her at her best. May was her soul sister."

I nod as I draw in another long breath and follow him up the porch steps. As he opens the door, I'm hit by a wave of all kinds of mouth-watering smells. Garlic, parsley, and a few other spices swirl in the air and remind me that we haven't eaten in a while. He pauses as he holds the door open for me.

"Mama's cookin' up a storm," he says with a shake of his head. "Her go-to move when she needs to keep busy."

As I follow him around the corner of the foyer and

into the kitchen, I feel the air escape from my lungs, and I suddenly feel my nerves standing on end. I've just followed a virtual stranger hundreds of miles from home to then walk inside of the house of yet another virtual stranger. To learn about my not-dead grandmother who is now, in fact, dead. And who was also a virtual stranger.

I see a short and stout woman with her back to us fiercely stirring something over the stove as she hums.

"Mama," he says, and she turns around. The first thing I think when I see Derrick's mom is that she's stunning. Her deep-brown skin is a little darker than Derrick's, but she has those same deep-brown eyes that he does. When our eyes meet, she lets out a long breath and slowly sets the wooden spoon down on the counter.

"She looks…" she whispers. Derrick clears his throat and nods.

"I know, Mama," he says. "I thought the same thing."

I give Derrick a look, and he shrugs. He leans in closer to me, and I notice my body responds immediately to his proximity.

"You look a *lot* like May," he says. I nod slowly.

"It's so nice to meet you, Kaylee. I'm Alma," she says, her voice cracking, just above a whisper. I see a tear well in her eye, and I'm surprised to feel them in my own, too. It feels like I just met someone I didn't realize I was missing. She takes a few steps toward me, and before I can prepare, she wraps me in a strong hug. I wrap my arms around her, and we stand like that for a few moments, soaking each other in.

"Shit," Derrick mutters from around us, scurrying to the stove to stir whatever is now boiling over.

"Oh, thank you, baby," she says, finally breaking her grasp on me and walking back over to the stove to resume making whatever it is that's making my stomach growl like a bear.

Then, she turns back to me.

"This must all be so confusing for you," she says to me. I nod, unsure of how else to respond. It *is* confusing. And no one seems to be ready to talk about it yet. "When Derrick said he wanted to go get you—" she says, and I freeze. I turn to Derrick, but his eyes drop to the ground.

"*You* wanted to come get me?" I ask him. He nods slowly.

"Yeah."

"I thought May wanted to see me," I say. He lets out a sigh.

"I think she did. She wasn't able to say much, but I know it cut her to the core that she couldn't say goodbye to you properly. Then and now. I just wanted to do right by her. And by you."

My eyes narrow on him, unsure of what he could possibly be doing right by me right now.

"Gosh, when I think of how close you were to meeting her again, to...oh, it just..." Alma's voice trails off, and a quiet sob catches in her throat. Derrick walks toward her and puts his hands on her shoulders, pulling her into him for a hug.

He's a big man, tall and broad, but he doesn't make you feel small.

When Alma collects herself again, Derrick reaches up into the cupboard above her head and pulls down three bowls.

"Mama's chili." He nods toward the big pot on the stove. "It's famous around here."

She swats at his shoulder.

"Not just around *here*, boy," she says before looking to me. "It's famous throughout the state."

I smile and nod.

"Well, I can't wait to try it," I tell her. She serves us, and I follow them out to the back porch where a small round table sits on the corner.

"So, have any arrangements been made?" Derrick asks her after we all dig in. I'm not sure if it's the malnourished trip I just took, but this chili really is good. Alma nods her head.

"Yeah, May had it all planned and paid for," she says. "Funeral will be in two days at Peake's Peak."

Derrick nods.

"Leave it to May to make this easier on us," he says. Then he turns to me. "Kaylee, do you wanna stay for the service?"

I swallow.

How do I say no to attending my own grandmother's funeral when everyone else in this town will be there?

I clear my throat and take a sip of my lemonade.

"Uh, yeah, I would like that," I say. He nods and gives me a soft smile, which is enough to make my stomach flip inside my body.

I know I should be thinking about my grandmother, but I'm not. I'm thinking about this beautiful, beautiful man in front of me. *Whew.* I snap back out of my Derrick trance when Alma speaks.

"Honey, you're welcome to stay here with me," she

says, "but if you're more comfortable, we can get you set up at the hotel."

Just as I'm struggling with how to respond, we hear voices from inside the house.

"Mama?" a man's voice calls.

"Out here," she says. I hear the scurrying of little feet running through the house, and suddenly, two young kids spill out onto the back deck, running for Alma. She scoops them both up into her lap, showering them with hugs and kisses, and I feel my heart swelling. When they're done with Alma, they make their way to Derrick, who does the same. And then I feel heat everywhere on my body.

A devilishly handsome man holding some kids? Goner, man. Goner.

"This is my niece, Kimora," he says, nuzzling the little girl's cheek and making her giggle. "And this is my nephew, Van." He squeezes the kids, tickling their sides and sending them into a fit of laughter before setting them back down. "Guys, say hi to Miss Kaylee. She...she knew Miss May."

Did she?

I smile faintly and say hi to them before they run off the porch and into the backyard. Just then, a man who looks a lot like Derrick appears at the back door, a woman appearing behind him, carrying a bowl of fruit. He's got a bit more going on in the gut area than Derrick does, and his face is definitely more aged. But it's no question they're related.

"This is my brother, Teddy, and my sister-in-law, Camille," Derrick tells me, holding his hand out toward them. "Ted, Cam, this...this is Kaylee."

They're both smiling, but as soon as they hear my

name, the smiles disappear. Their eyes widen as they look from Derrick to Alma, to me, and back to Derrick. I follow their path, trying to see what it is they're seeing.

"Kaylee...like...May's Kaylee?" Teddy asks. Derrick nods. "Wow, I, uh, it's nice to meet you, Kaylee. I'm, uh, sorry for your...loss?" he says it like a question, and I actually can't help but chuckle out loud.

When I realize everyone is staring at me, I clear my throat and straighten myself out.

"I'm sorry," I say, feeling my cheeks flush. "I know it's no laughing matter. I guess this is all just...well, it's really freakin' weird. You have to excuse me, but I'm having trouble mourning her right now. In my world, she's been dead for two decades."

"It's nice to meet you, Kaylee," Camille says before awkwardly slipping off the porch to follow the kids into the yard.

Alma leans back in her chair and gives me a half-smile.

"Don't apologize, baby," she says. "There's a lot going on here. This is all very...strange. It will make more sense soon. We just need to talk—"

She's cut off by the sound of more feet walking through the house. The sliding door opens again, and out comes a strikingly gorgeous woman with chestnut-brown hair tied into a loose braid over her shoulder. She's holding a platter of meats and cheeses, and she's got a little girl clinging to her leg. They're followed by a man who's also strikingly beautiful—Jesus, what is in the water up here?—who is using a walking stick as he makes his way across the deck. Derrick hops up and makes his way to them, kissing both the woman and the girl on the cheeks and pulling the man in for a hug.

"I can't believe it, man," the man whispers. Derrick leads him to the table and pulls out a chair for him. As I watch him feel his way around the table, I realize the man can't see.

"Kaylee, this is my very best friend in the world, Ryder Casey," he says, clapping Ryder on the shoulder. Ryder looks up to him.

"Kaylee?" he whispers. Does *everyone* here know who I am? But Derrick goes on.

"And his lovely soon-to-be wife, Mila. And this," he says, bending down to scoop up the little girl, "is my girl, Annabelle."

She giggles and wraps her arms around his neck before he sets her back down to go play with Van and Kimora.

Ugh. My ovaries.

Suddenly, the house erupts in loud, boisterous conversation. They are actually laughing and smiling some, eating all the food and drinking. A few more cars pull up, and I am getting used to the way people just walk right in, knowing they are needed here at this time. They need to be together. And it's beautiful. I watch as Derrick introduces me, one by one, and I see how their eyes all widen. The whole time, Derrick doesn't leave my side. He gets me refills, makes sure I've had enough to eat, and tells me story after story about May.

While they're all great company so far, I have to admit, I'm feeling socially exhausted. It's hard meeting person after person, especially knowing that they are clued in to the mess that is my family more than I am myself.

As I stand to begin to say my goodbyes and casually

mention that I'm going to get a hotel room for the night, the back door slides open again.

Out steps a tall, slim, young woman with skin a bit lighter than Derrick's. Her hair is dark, wild, beautiful curls bouncing together with each step she takes. Her face is carrying something heavy; it's pained. And as she turns back to face us from closing the door, I notice that everyone has gone silent. All eyes are on her. But she scans the crowd, and then her eyes land on me.

As she narrows them in on me, her jaw drops, and she turns her glare to Derrick.

"I can't believe you," she whispers to him, her bottom lip starting to tremble.

"Oh, baby," Alma says, standing slowly from the table. Derrick stands, too, his eyes on her, his chest heaving up and down. He takes a few steps toward her, but she steps away from him and puts her hand out. Alma makes her way up next to me, keeping her eyes trained on Derrick and the woman, as if deciding when she needs to intervene.

"She never got the letters," I hear Derrick say in sort of a loud whisper.

I can't quite make out what the woman is saying to Derrick, but I can practically feel the heat radiating from their conversation. His voice remains low and calm, but hers is high and frantic. Filled with emotion. Filled with pain. Alma steps up to them, standing between them and trying to diffuse whatever situation is going on. Except, I'm starting to get the feeling that *I* am the situation.

I feel a nudge up against me, and I turn to see Mila next to me.

"Hey," she says, "while they're dealing with that, can

I get you something else to eat?" I turn slowly to her and smile.

"Oh, um, sure," I say, reluctantly turning back to the table.

"Don't mind them," she says, using tongs to put a few more pieces of cheese on my plate. "Family matters."

I turn back to them then back to her.

"Is that his sister?" I ask just as everyone around me is quiet. I swallow the piece of cheese I'm chewing and turn back to Derrick, Alma, and the mystery woman who would have one hundred percent won any modeling show on television. The woman scoffs and crosses her arms over her chest, jutting a hip out. She glares at Derrick as she pushes past him, then her eyes find me.

"Actually," she says, "I'm yours."

5

It's so quiet all I can hear is the engine of a distant boat and the shriek of the kids playing in the grass below. I look at the woman, my eyes narrowed on hers. I study every inch of her face; I study her bone structure, her lips. She can't be much older than high school age, but there's something about her that makes her seem older, more worldly, like she's seen a lot.

I'm looking for answers in her eyes, but similar to everything else that's happened in the last few hours, all I'm getting is more questions.

I look to Alma, who has dropped her head and closed her eyes. I look to Mila, whose eyes are big and filled with worry. And then I find Derrick, who is staring at me.

"What is she...what is she talking about?" I ask him just above a whisper.

"Kaylee——" he says, but I shake my hand.

"It's a two-for-one deal on dead relatives that aren't really dead," the girl says. "Nice to meet ya, *sis.*"

Then she disappears back into the house.

I look around again, frantic now, waiting for someone—*anyone*—on this deck to tell me it's not true. That this girl is crazy. But no one will look at me. I slowly back away, one step at a time. I set my cup down and look at each of them then take a step off the deck.

"Kaylee, please," Derrick starts to say, taking a step closer, but I hold my hand up, warning him to stay back.

What the fuck did I get myself into?

I back away slowly, and once I gain my footing on the gravel driveway, I turn, and I run. I run past my own car in his driveway. I turn down the street like I know where the fuck I'm going. I follow the curve and inclines of the road, up and down, jagged and unpredictable, until I come to the crest of a hill. I hear brakes squeak next to me, and the dull roar of a stalling engine.

"Runnin' all the way back to Georgia?" Mila asks me. I'm huffing and puffing, beads of sweat starting to form on my brow. I'm panting like a dog, but she's just rolling along next to me, her perfect, angelic face turned toward me as she creeps along the road. Finally, I give up and come to a stop, and she does the same, pulling the truck over just in front of me. She hops out and walks toward me. I catch my breath and look at her.

"What the fuck is up with this place?" I ask her. She stares at me for a moment then chuckles.

"I've had similar thoughts," she says. "But the truth is, this place gave me my life. This place…and the people in it."

I hear her, but I'm not really soaking it in. I'm a little distracted by the fact that my sister—who I *also* thought was dead—is, in fact, alive. And that the sister I always pictured—my doppelganger, with blonde hair and fair skin—never seemed to exist in the first place.

"None of this makes any damn sense," I say, crossing my arms over my chest. "I don't even know these people." Mila gives me a look and leans back on her hip.

"It sounds to me like maybe you don't know the people who raised you," she says matter-of-factly. There's a long pause for a moment, and then she speaks. "Look, from one outsider to another, can I give you some advice?"

I give her a reluctant nod.

"Don't write them off. The people here in Meade Lake are some of the best people I've ever known, your grandmother included. Maybe take some time and get a little space. I can take you to this little bed and breakfast on the other side of the lake that I stayed at when I first got here. Take the night to decide if you want to find out who you really are, or if you want to leave. But take the night. Deal?"

I think for a moment then nod. We get in her truck, and I see she already has my bag.

"I grabbed it from Derrick before I followed you. In case you did opt not to go back," she says with a shrug as she pulls back onto the road.

"What did...what did Derrick say?" I ask.

"He wanted to come after you himself," she says. "But being that he's the one that *brought* you into this, I thought maybe someone else could give you a ride." She smiles, and I smile back. There's something soothing about Mila.

The thought of Derrick coming after me makes my stomach dance. I can't believe how much like a lusting teenager he makes me feel.

"He's, uh, not hard to look at, huh?" Mila asks, and for a second, I think I've said it out loud.

"Huh?"

"Derrick," she says. "Easy on the eyes."

I nod slowly, not wanting to give too much away. She smiles.

"Don't tell Ryder I said this—actually, he would agree—Derrick is the best man I've ever met. We would have been lost without him this last year."

I want to ask her for more, but I realize that I haven't known her longer than a few hours. We drive in silence for a few more minutes before she turns left onto another long, wooded road. I can see the lake behind some trees, and a beautiful Victorian house sits nestled on the shore a few yards ahead of us. She pulls the truck into the driveway and puts it in park. I turn to her.

"How much do you know about me? About that...woman?" I ask her. She swallows and keeps her eyes trained on the road.

"Enough," she says. "But I can't be the one to tell you, Kaylee. I'm sorry." I nod.

More fucking secrets.

"Can you just tell me...is that girl really my sister?" I whisper. Mila takes in a deep breath and looks up at me, her long lashes curling out.

"Yes," she says.

"But she's..." I say.

"Black," Mila says, nodding. "Yeah, she is." She reaches over and squeezes my hand, gently letting me know that this conversation is over. She grabs my bag and hops out of the truck. I take another deep breath and follow her into the house. She introduces me to the older woman behind the desk.

"Sue, this is Kaylee; she's a friend from out of

town," Mila tells her. "Can she have a room for the night?"

"Absolutely," Sue says, clapping her hands together.

Sue has us sign in an old book on the desk then hands me a room key.

"Last door on your right up the steps, darlin'," she says. I thank her and pick up my bag. I look around and see one other person out on the deck, but other than that, the place seems empty.

"Ever since the Willington Ski Resort opened a few years back, the rest of the inns around here have had some trouble filling up," she says. "I always try to bring people here when they're in from out of town."

I nod and smile.

"This will be perfect," I tell her. "Thanks, Mila."

She smiles.

"I recognized that lost look in you," she says. "I had it myself not so long ago. But I found what I needed here. Maybe you will, too."

She leaves, and I go up to my room and lay my things out. I change into some comfy yoga pants, grab a sweat jacket, and walk back down the stairs. I go onto the back deck and look out over the water. It's orange, streaked with what's left of the sun in the sky as it slips down behind the black and green mountains in front of me.

It's beautiful here.

I lean back against the chaise lounge and breathe in…and out. In…and out. My phone buzzing at my side jolts me out of this nature-induced meditation I've slipped into.

When I see my dad's name pop up, I freeze.

In just twenty-four hours, I've learned so much—

and yet, so little—about my parents. And though I don't know all the details, I know that, for the last twenty years, they've lied to me. I hit *decline* and wait for his text to come in.

He's used to me answering every call, every text.

I'm Daddy's sweetheart and the heiress to his big ol' technology throne.

Never much more than a stone's throw away.

Even in college, he'd set me up on lunches with well-connected professors and, at one point, even the dean.

His pull seemed to have no end, and I had no choice but to oblige. After all, that tuition bill would not be a fun one to pay back one day.

Like clockwork, the text pops up.

Where ya at, kiddo?

I type, and stop, type, and stop. I can't answer him right now.

After a few more minutes of breathing in the mountain air, my hands slowly stop trembling. I feel an overwhelming sense of peace.

I don't know what I'm going to find while I'm here, but I know I need to find it.

6

I wake up the next morning feeling refreshed. I haven't slept that well in, well, ever. I roll out of the bed and walk to the mirror, running my fingers through my long blonde locks, and tug on a pair of jean shorts.

As I walk down the creaky staircase into the main foyer, I can smell cinnamon from the kitchen. I walk across, but I stop when I hear his voice.

"You stayed," Derrick says, standing up from the couch in the living room. I swallow as he makes his way toward me. "I was worried you might have…"

There's a long, awkward pause. He's got on a t-shirt that fits snug around his muscles and jeans. The sight of him makes my insides sink and my heart rate quicken. I shouldn't be this hot and bothered this early in the morning.

"Well, I kind of don't have a car," I say. He smiles and shrugs.

"True," he says. "Do you want that back, by the way?"

"That might be helpful," I say with a flirty smile. I don't quite know what to make of Derrick. I can't deny that my body reacts to him. But my mind does, too. I want to know more of him. I want to listen to him, make him laugh.

But he's also the one who brought me here when no one else seemed to have thought that was a good idea.

"Mama wanted me to come see if you wouldn't mind having a talk with her today," he says. I look at him, skeptical. "Just the two of you. No one else will be there."

I wait a beat then nod.

"I'd like that," I say.

"Good. I also came by because I wanted to make sure you were alright."

I swallow.

"You tell me," I say. He gives me a look of confusion. "Everyone else seems to know everything there is to know about Kaylee Jennings, except for Kaylee Jennings herself."

He blows out a long breath and rubs the back of his head.

"Yeah, I bet it does feel like that. It'll make more sense when you talk to Mama today. She's got the answers. Most of 'em, anyway," he says. "Wanna get some breakfast and I'll take you over to her place?"

I think for a minute, chewing on my lip as I narrow my eyes at him.

There are a lot of reasons why a sane person wouldn't trust him. Wouldn't keep putting herself in a position to be made a fool of, and lied to, and hidden from.

But he flashes me that panty-dropping half-smile,

and I know I can no longer consider myself sane—if I ever did in the first place.

I nod and follow him out the door. He opens the passenger door for me, and the little acts of chivalry don't cease to amaze me.

"How'd you sleep?" he asks as we start down the road.

"Well, actually."

"Good," he says. "That mountain air will do that to ya."

"Yeah, either that or being in the land of undead relatives."

He throws his head back and laughs, and the sound makes my stomach flip.

"Sorry, I know it's not funny, but…"

"It's kind of funny," I say with a giggle. He pulls off Lake Shore Highway a few minutes later and into the parking lot of a small diner. We go inside, and he leans over the counter, batting his eyes at the ladies behind it.

"Mornin', Bette," he says, and he's got the charm turned all the way up.

"Hey, cutie," an older woman says as she makes her way to him. He smiles at her, and they make small talk while the woman asks about Alma and says how sorry she is that May is gone. Without realizing it, I clear my throat at the back of the restaurant.

Just as he's turning to me, another woman comes from behind the counter. She's younger, probably close to our age. And when she reaches her hands up to tie her hair into a bun, her shirt lifts a little, exposing her tanned and toned midriff. I feel that heat raging through me again in the form of jealousy.

But Derrick's eyes never falter from hers.

"Hey, D," she says, walking toward him and reaching her arms around his neck to pull him down into a hug. Her breasts push up against him, but he doesn't seem to notice.

"Hey, Kat," he says, "good to see you." She looks up at him with twinkling fuck-me eyes, batting her eyelashes, seemingly unaware of anyone else in the diner. He clears his throat after a moment and holds his arm out to me. I take a few steps forward, and her face drops.

"This is my friend Kaylee," he says. "She's from out of town. I wanted to get her Meade Lake's best breakfast." He turns back to Bette and winks. She winks back.

"Well, you know you came to the right place, honey," she says. "Be right up." Derrick leads me to two chairs in the middle of the diner where we sit to wait for our food.

"What did we order?" I ask. He smiles.

"She makes homemade apple doughnuts," he says. "They're out of this world." My mouth waters.

"Yum," I say. I look back toward the counter and see Kat eyeing us down. "Maybe I should scoot over some so your friend doesn't try to kill me with her eyes."

He looks up at her then back down to his hands, smiling and shaking his head.

"Kat, she's a friend. Moved here a few years ago. But she's just—"

"Order's ready, honey," Bette calls, and Derrick walks to the front to pay the bill and pick it up. I reach for my wallet, but he holds up his hand to decline it.

"You're our guest," he says before pushing the door open and leading me back out to the truck. The apple doughnut melts in my mouth, and I hum with satisfaction at the first bite. He laughs.

"Good, huh?" he asks.

"Mmm," I respond before taking another bite. Before I realize it, I've eaten the whole thing. He looks at me from the driver's seat, crumpling up the paper the doughnut was wrapped in and dropping it in his cup holder. He does a double-take and looks back to me again just as we pull up to a stop light.

He leans over the center console, and I feel my breath catch as I realize he's getting closer. I swallow as he reaches a hand out toward my face. Then he sticks his thumb out and swipes my bottom lip gently.

"Got a little icing," he says then puts his hands back on the steering wheel. I swallow and tuck a piece of hair behind my ear.

"Thanks. So, um, do you live with your mom?" I ask him as we drive farther down Lake Shore Highway.

"Nah," he says, shaking his head. "I have a place up on the top of that mountain." He points to the giant mountain to our right, carved with ski slopes and dotted by thousands of trees.

I nod.

"I'll give you the official Meade Lake tour after you talk to Mama," he says. "Assuming you want to stick around, that is."

He gives me that devilish half-smile again, and I feel that tingle that starts in my belly and goes down.

After a few more minutes, we pull into Alma's driveway. I draw in a long breath and reach for my door handle. But before I open it, he does from the outside. As I turn to get out, he takes a step closer to me, putting his hands on the seat on either side of me. He leans in close.

"Hey," he says just above a whisper. I look up at him, my eyes catching his. "It's gonna be okay."

I narrow my eyes and nod. I don't know if I believe him, but I do know that I feel better when he's around.

He leads me inside.

"Mama," he calls as we walk through the door. "We're here!"

Alma makes her way down the hall from the bedrooms toward the foyer to greet us.

"Hi, baby," she says to me. "I'm so glad we didn't scare you off. I know yesterday was a bit much. I have some coffee made. I thought we could sit outside on the deck and talk."

I smile and nod.

"That would be great." Alma grabs two mugs off the counter and walks out the back door onto the deck.

Derrick nods in my direction and tips an imaginary hat.

"I'll leave you to it," he says. "We'll catch up later."

"You're not staying?" I ask before I realize how needy it makes me sound. But the truth is, I *do* feel like I need him right now. He's my only clarity here, despite the fact that he tracked me down and brought me here in the first place. He smiles.

"Mama doesn't bite," he says. "I gotta get into the shop for a few. But I'll be back to check in on you."

My stomach flips again.

"What shop?" I ask. He clears his throat.

"Uh, there's a little shop on the highway. Boat rentals and things like that. Nothing special," he says with a modest shrug. "I'll see you later. Don't leave." He winks at me as he walks out the door, and I feel my palms get instantly clammy.

Don't leave. I do like the idea. Except for the company I'm supposed to be taking over. The parents who are counting on me.

I walk out onto the deck and squint in the early morning sunlight. Alma unwinds the table umbrella, and we sit down.

"I have cream and sugar here on the table if you need it," she says.

"Thanks, but I actually drink it black." Her eyes get wide. "What?"

"Nothin'," she says, "it's just that May took it black, too." I take a big gulp of the scalding coffee and nod. "So, where should we start?"

I smile.

"I was hoping you could tell me." She smiles back and leans back in her chair.

"Well, why don't we start by you telling me what you remember about your Gran May and your sister."

I swallow and nod. It's been a long time since anyone wanted me to remember May or the baby. It's been a long time since I've been *allowed* to talk about either.

"Okay, sure. Um, when I was five, my mom was pregnant. I remember going to the hospital the morning the baby was born. I was in the waiting room with Gran May for a while. I remember she gave me this little music box that had a baby on it." I smile, and my heart wrenches. "I remember my dad finally came out from the back, and then he left the hospital. And then all I remember is I never met the baby, and Gran May died—or, I guess, *didn't* die?—shortly after. I never saw either of them again after that day in the hospital."

Alma nods.

"And what did your parents say?"

"Um, well, I remember a little while later, my mom told me that my baby sister died in the hospital that day. And she told me that Gran May died, too, of a broken heart."

Alma's lip trembles a bit, and she catches it with her hand.

"I'm sorry, Alma," I say. "I don't mean to speak so candidly about her dying. I know she just passed and this is a lot for you."

She smiles a pained smile and covers my hand with hers.

"No, baby, don't you apologize. These are more tears of anger than anything else, I'm afraid," she says. I swallow. "So, your mama was pregnant. She did have a baby. But that baby did not die, and neither did your Gran May. I'm sure you noticed the other day that Haven is a bit, uh, on the darker side?"

I pause.

Haven.

"Is that her name? Haven?" I ask. Alma nods slowly.

"Yes, honey. May said she looked at her that day they moved up here, and she knew she was safe."

I swallow the lump that's growing in my throat.

"I love that name," I whisper. "And yes, I had noticed she was a little darker than I am."

"A little," Alma says, eyeing my fair skin and winking. "As you might have guessed, your mama was pregnant, but your father was not *the* father. Haven's dad was black."

My head spins a little.

I knew it had to be an affair. There's not a Caucasian person in the world that could produce the beautiful brown skin tone or those gorgeous textured curls that made me envious the moment I laid eyes on her. But my mother? My quiet, complacent, "yes sir," mother?

"Who was it?" I ask. Alma shrugs.

"None of us know to this day," she says. "Just one more thing your mama took from her." My eyes grow wide, and so do Alma's. "I'm sorry, honey. I promised myself I wouldn't go harpin' on your mama. But I just—"

"No, it's okay. So, what happened?"

"Well, your dad was in the room, and after they got the baby all cleaned up, it was pretty obvious she wasn't, uh, his. Some biracial children are born fair and get darker as they age. But with Haven, she was beautifully brown the day she was born."

I nod.

"Your dad put it together before your mother was even out of the delivery room. Gave her an ultimatum."

Oh, God.

"An ultimatum?"

"Yes. Her option was to give the baby up or give *him* up. I guess you can see which your mama picked."

I feel nauseous.

"So, May…"

"When your father stormed out that day, May went back in to see your mom. She thought something had happened, only to find your mama filling out some paperwork to relinquish guardianship rights. She stopped her mid-sign and told her that she was taking the baby."

Oh, God. It's all coming together.

"So, how did they end up here?"

"Well, your mother refused to sign over guardianship unless May agreed to leave Georgia and cut off all ties. Your parents conjured up a story about their deaths and told everyone she wanted to be buried up here in Meade Lake where her uncle had lived."

"Her uncle?"

"Yeah. May's uncle was in oil way back when. The house she and Haven lived in here was his. He didn't have children and left it to her when he died."

I nod, trying to follow along.

"After the court hearings for final guardianship rights, May took Haven and left. And your parents took you and moved a few hours away to Lenburn shortly after. I suspect it was too big of a lie for them to uphold around the people that knew them."

I lay my head back against the chair, staring up at the puffy clouds that are dancing across the bluest sky I've ever seen.

"So, all that brings us to you," Alma goes on. I snap my head back.

"Me?" She nods.

"Part of the agreement was that May was permitted to reach out to you when you turned eighteen. And she did try."

I cock my head.

"She did?"

"Yes," Alma says, her eyes dropping to the ground. "It seems as though those attempts were, um, inter-cepted, baby. When Derrick came to find you, he thought you'd been ignoring her letters. Angry, maybe, that she abandoned you." I pause. *Am I angry that she abandoned me?* "He knew it was a shot in the dark, and even though a few of us were apprehensive, he wanted to do it for May."

I swallow.

"Apprehensive?" I ask.

"Yeah, honey. That brings me to the next piece of this puzzle that is your life." She walks into the house for a moment and then walks back out with a manila envelope tucked under her arm. "This here is May's will. May's lawyer, Jeffrey, is on his way to walk you through it."

Like clockwork, the house fills with a sing-song voice calling out Alma's name.

"We're out here, Jeff!" she calls. He follows her voice to the sliding glass doors and makes his way onto the deck.

He's tall and slim and slender, wearing a perfectly tailored suit despite the warm summer

weather. His square jaw is clean-shaven, and his hair is combed and styled perfectly on top of his head.

"Oh, my *God,*" he says, staring me up and down. He walks toward me and takes my hands, pulling me up from the chair. He spins me around then takes my face in his hands before pulling me into his chest. I choke on his cologne as he slowly lets me go.

"You are her spitting image," he whispers, covering his mouth with his hands. I smile.

"So I've been told," I say. "I'm Kaylee."

"Jeffrey Tate," he says. "I've been May's attorney for twenty years. It is damn good to finally meet you, Kaylee."

Jeff turns to Alma as he takes a seat at the table with us.

"Paul is going to die when he sees her," he says. Then he turns back to me. "My husband and May were close. And he's just going to fall apart when he sees you. It's like she's still here."

I shift uncomfortably in my seat and force a smile.

I'm not May. I can't be her for them.

Alma slides the envelope over to me and clears her throat.

"I was just getting to the part of the story about why a few of us had some, uh, concerns about Kaylee coming up here." Jeff's eyes widen as he opens the folder.

"Oh, yes. Cue Jeffrey," he says.

7

Jeffrey reaches into his briefcase and pulls out a stack of papers. On the front cover, it reads: WILL AND TESTAMENT OF MAY DEAN.

I swallow.

"That's your copy. You can follow along with me," he says, turning the page. I do the same.

My eyes scan the paper in front of me, top to bottom, left to right. So many big words that they bleed together in front of my eyes.

"So, basically, a lot of this is a bunch of gobble-de-gook," Jeffrey says. "Let me get to the point: your Gran May was loaded."

My eyes grow wide.

"Loaded?"

He nods.

"*Loaded.* Turns out her uncle still had a not-so-small fortune from his years in oil. He left the house to May, but he also left her every penny he had—which was an insane amount, if I'm not being too frank. Her will indicates that the money and house be split between her two beneficiaries: Haven Dean and you."

I blink wildly. I look from Jeffrey, to the paper where he's pointing to my name, to Alma, back to the paper.

"*Me?*" Jeffrey nods slowly. "But she didn't even know me."

Alma clears her throat.

"When your Gran May got her diagnosis, she sat us all down and walked us through her plans. She told us that she left you once, but she wouldn't leave you again."

I feel this lump rising in my throat. A strange mix of anxiety, excitement, and confusion swirl in my stomach, making me nauseous.

"This is the estimated asset amount," Jeffrey says, flipping to the next page. "Some of her investments are still being compiled and calculated, but this is pretty close."

My eyes bug out of my head when I see the number.

"This is what will be split between you and your sister," Alma clarifies. I look back at the thick black ink —so many numbers trailed by *so* many zeros.

"So...is that why you all were a little hesitant to bring me up here? If I hadn't come, would she...would Haven have gotten all of it?" I ask.

Alma looks to Jeffrey, who looks back to me. He shakes his head.

"No. Haven would only get half of the money regardless of if you ever came up here to claim yours." I cock my head, confused. "Your Gran May was a bit of a businesswoman here in Meade Lake. When the recession hit, a lot of the businesses around here took major hits. A lot of them closed their doors forever. Some held on by a thread. May recognized that the entire economy of the town was in jeopardy, so she began a sort of investment program."

"An investment program?"

He nods.

"She began working with the small business owners. She gave them small loans to get them back up and running, and it worked. I guess 'investment' isn't the right word; she only took back what she put in but left all the remaining profit to the businesses themselves."

"She singlehandedly saved this town from being swallowed up whole," Alma says. "When the recession hit, people stopped coming on vacations for a while. Everything was stagnant. When the town started moving again with the help of May, and once the recession was over, she started helping out new business owners who wanted a shot."

"That's...that's amazing," I say, feeling the emotion threatening to manifest itself as tears again. "But what does that have to do with me coming here?"

"Well, when May tried to contact you and failed, she had a stipulation added to the will regarding your portion of the inheritance." Jeff turns a few pages in the document and does the same on my copy. He taps his finger on another bunch of really big words. "What this says is that if you didn't come up here to claim your half by the time Haven graduated from college, two years from now, you would forfeit your right to your half. That money would then go into a fund that would be dispersed to local businesses."

"So, if I hadn't come…"

"If you hadn't come, the money would be sitting for the next three years but would be guaranteed to be funneled back into the local economy."

"So, what's happening to those businesses right now?" I ask.

"May set aside enough money for the ones she's actively lending money to to get them through the next fiscal year," Jeffrey says. "She set up the fund so that you and Haven could easily continue her 'program,' but it's not a requirement of finalizing the inheritance."

It makes sense now why Haven wouldn't have wanted me to come.

They thought I was ignoring May's attempts at contacting me. And now, here I am, showing up to steal her money and leave the town out to dry.

"Now, if you determine that you'd like to continue lending money to these businesses, there's a complete ledger in this file that will show you who she is lending money to, how much, and how much of the original loan has been paid back. You'll see that some haven't begun the repayment process; May was quite generous and didn't really have a timeline requirement for when she wanted the money back," Jeffrey says.

My head is spinning. Last week, I cleaned out my closet and threw away an old container of green lasagna that was rotting in the back of my fridge. And I thought *that* was a productive week.

This week, I've discovered not one, but *two* not-dead relatives, found out I'm a millionaire, and basically am the key to the success of the storybook little town I've landed in.

"We know this is a lot, honey," Alma says.

"Absolutely. You don't have to make any decisions right now," Jeffrey says. "There's just one more thing to go over."

He reaches into the front pocket of his briefcase and

pulls out a set of keys. He slides them across the table to me.

"That fob there is to May's Explorer. Haven has her own car, so the Explorer is yours if you want it," he says. "And the silver one is to the house. *Your* house. Well, yours and Haven's."

I swallow.

"Haven is going to stay with me for a few days," Alma says, "so we can take you to the house if you want to see it."

"I hope she doesn't feel like she has to get out," I say.

"Oh, don't worry, *she* doesn't," a cool voice says from the door, and it makes me jump. Her curls sit nestled around her face, and I'm instantly envious of the beauty she exudes. She doesn't appear to have a drop of make-up on, but she doesn't have a blemish or spot on her skin. Her eyes are piercing in the sunlight, and her brown skin glows under her flowy tank top.

"Haven," Alma says.

"Hey, Haven," Jeffrey greets her, his cheerful demeanor fading a bit.

I've now officially seen her only twice. But I've already come to one conclusion: Haven commands eyes. Her body language and the ferocity she carries with her demand attention. She's bold and on a mission. And if getting rid of me weren't that mission, I think I'd actually really want to get to know her.

"We were just finishing up," Alma says. Jeffrey takes her cue and closes his files.

"Well, Kaylee, you have a copy of everything there in that file. Take a look through it, and here's my card if you have any questions about anything." He bends across the table to kiss Alma's cheek. "I'll see you ladies at the funeral."

I nod and stand.

"Thank you, Jeffrey. It was really nice to meet you," I say. He gives my hand a squeeze then ducks back through the door.

My eyes drift from the door to Alma then to Haven. She's staring at me, her eyes narrowed.

"Jeffrey fill you in? Don't have to even be a part of the family or the town and get to walk outta here with millions," she says, leaning up against the deck railing.

"Haven," Alma cautions.

"I didn't come here to take anything from anyone," I tell her. "I didn't even know there was money."

Haven scoffs and crosses her arms.

"But I bet you're thinking about leaving with it, huh?" she asks. I swallow. Because truthfully, I don't even know what I'm doing. I just found out an hour ago that I am a very, very wealthy woman.

I just found out a half-hour ago that part of that wealth has been put into programs to help out small businesses and improve the lives of hundreds of people.

I feel this burning sense of pride and awe over May. Programs like these are ones I'd researched in my sociology courses in college and had recommended to my dad to implement at Jennings Technology. Not shockingly, nothing had ever come of them. My dad has tunnel vision, and the only thing he sees is a dollar sign.

"Cut her some slack, Hay," I hear Derrick say as he walks around from the front of the house. He climbs the deck steps and stands next to me. "You've known about her your whole life. She *just* found out about you and all of this," he says, motioning to the file, "this week."

Haven narrows her eyes on Derrick.

"Yeah? And she wouldn't have known about it at all if you hadn't gone down there."

"You know it's what May would have wanted," Derrick says, and Haven's eyes widen. There's a long, tense silence, and then I push my chair out to stand.

"I think I'm gonna…" My voice trails off because I don't really know what I'm going to do. I guess I could go back to my room at the B&B and figure out some things there.

"I was actually coming by to see if you wanted that tour of Meade Lake," Derrick says. He looks up at Alma. "Assuming you're all done here?"

Alma nods.

"I think that's enough of a knowledge dump for the day," she chuckles, rubbing my arm.

"Thank you, Alma, for filling me in on everything," I tell her. I turn to Derrick. "That tour sounds great."

8

———

He opens the truck door for me every time I get in with him, and each time, it makes my heart skip a beat or two.

"Looks like I got there at just the right time," he says with a laugh as he pulls on his seatbelt. I blow out a big puff of air that makes my hair fly up.

"I don't even know what to say," I say, running my hands over my face as we pull out onto the road.

"You don't have to say anything at all," he says, his voice warm. "You just got two decades worth of family secrets dumped on you. You're good for a while, girl. Just soak it all in."

He flashes me that perfectly white grin, and I feel my own lips tug up into a smile. The whole time I sat at Alma's, my stomach was turning into tight knots. I felt nauseous, my palms clammy as I turned the pages in sync with Jeff.

But after one minute in this truck with him, I feel myself let out the breath I'd been holding. I feel myself letting go and letting it all settle inside me.

I turn and look out the window, staring up at the sea of green we're driving through. At the end of the road, the trees clear a bit, and as he pulls onto Lake Shore Highway, I can see the blue of the water.

"Not a lot of wind today, so it's not too choppy," he says. "Whattya say?"

I turn to him and cock my head.

"About what?"

He nods his head toward the water as he drives down the highway.

"The best way to see the town is by water," he says with a shrug and a devilish smile. I look out at the lake again.

"Let's do it," I say. He nods and picks up speed, and after a few more minutes on the windy highway, he pulls off into a parking lot in front of a small strip of stores and shops. "Where are we?"

"Just gotta get the key," he says. He takes the keys out of the ignition and pulls one from the chain. He hops out and walks over to one of the shop doors. Above it hangs a huge sign that says *Big Moon Sports*. I follow behind him and look around the store. There are spinning racks of clothes and bathing suits, sunglasses, huge inner tubes hanging on the wall, water skis hanging from the ceiling.

"Do you work here?" I ask him as he walks behind the front counter and uses another key on his chain to get into a glass case. He pulls another key from the glass and closes it then stuffs it in his pocket. He chuckles.

"Uh, yeah. You could say that," he says. "Come on, let's go."

I follow him out the door of the shop. He locks it and holds a hand out for me to cross the parking lot. We wait on the side of Lakeshore Highway for the traffic to clear then swiftly walk across the crosswalk. He leads me down a set of questionable wooden steps then onto a set of docks. There's a small shed on one of the docks, and boats and jet skis are tied to them on either side. I follow him down the longest dock to a speedboat, and he turns to me and holds out a hand.

I look up at him. His brown eyes are big and gleaming, and one corner of his mouth is tugged up into a grin. It's breezy this close to the water, and when it blows my hair back off my shoulders, it sends a chill down my spine. I smile back at him and slip my hand into his. The stark contrast of my flesh on his makes me pause for a moment, the sunlight bouncing off of my porcelain skin while it seeps into the darkness of his. I step up onto the back of the boat and sink down into the passenger seat.

He hops on and unties the boat then uses his foot to push us off. He sits down in the driver's seat and starts the boat using the key he got from the store, and we're off. As he pulls out into the water, he hops up to pull the buoys in. He grabs one on his side of the boat, and I hop up to grab the one on mine. As I stand back up, I catch his eyes on my backside for half a second. I bite my lip as I slide back down into my seat.

"Nah," he says just as my butt touches the leather. I look at him quizzically. "You get the best view from up there." He points to the seat at the nose of the boat. I smile at him as I stand slowly.

"Okay," I say, "but try to not stare again." I raise my eyebrows at him playfully, but the look on his face is a little less playful. He clears his throat as I shimmy past him and up to the front of the boat.

I kneel on the soft cushions of the front seat and look out over the water. There are boats whizzing by us, water skiers making it look completely effortless, families fishing off of distant docks.

The wind gets stronger as he picks up speed, and I grab hold of the railings on either side of me.

"Relax," he says. "You're fairly safe with me."

I look back at him and narrow my eyes.

"'Fairly?'" I say with a smile. He chuckles, and my stomach flips. His gaze intensifies a bit, and I bite my lip in response.

"I've been driving boats on this water since I was twelve," he says. "I got you."

I nod and turn forward, pushing my long honey locks off my shoulders and letting them fall to my back. I close my eyes and gently let my head drop back as he points the nose of the boat toward the big, open heart of Meade Lake.

All I feel is the rumbling of the water below us. All I hear is the moaning of the engine and the wind whipping past my ears. But I feel his eyes on me, and that has my spine straight and heart skipping a beat.

"So, if you'll look to your right," he says with his best tour-guide voice, "that's Lou's Lakeside Grille. Lou was a close friend of May. Best burgers in Meade Lake." I smile and nod as I look up at the bar on the shore. Another wooden staircase leads up to it from the docks. It has a big deck with string lights on the back, and it's packed.

We move a little farther up the shoreline.

"That there is the B&B you're staying at," he says. I nod, looking at it from the water. It's such a cute little inn, the perfect place to escape to after all I've learned today.

He veers left down a cove and slows down a bit.

"We all call this Rich Man's Cove," he says with a smile. "And you can probably see why."

My jaw drops when I see them. Massive, castle-like houses with perfectly manicured yards. Some with pools. All with impeccable boats tied down to their massive docks. One has a tennis court; another has a guest house.

"Wow," I mutter, still ogling. He laughs.

"Yeah," he says. "Crazy thing is, these people don't even live here year-round. These are just vacation homes."

"My God," I say. "Can you imagine having that much money?"

Then we both grow quiet.

I swallow and look back toward him sheepishly.

"You might be able to more than I can now," he says with a smile.

Oh, yeah. I forgot. I'm a millionaire now.

He spins the boat back around and pulls back down the cove, veering to the left. As we make our way into the wide mouth of the lake, I hear laughter, screaming, and loud music in the distance. I look up ahead and see a massive building perched on the shoreline at the base of a big building behind it. Sand covers the shore in front of it, and people are laying out and playing volleyball. Ski lifts trail up the mountain behind it, and "Willington" is painted down the side of the building in huge, gold letters.

"What is that?" I ask. Derrick scoffs.

"The Willington. The soul-sucker of all small businesses here in Meade Lake." I narrow my eyes at him. "It popped up a few years ago when the Willington family bought the land when the original owner died. Four-season resort. Complete with its own private mountain, private beach, and two four-star restaurants. They also have a ski shop and a cafe, so pretty much, something to rival every single business in the area."

I nod. I'm not used to the disdain I hear in his voice. I swallow, thinking about my father and Jennings Technology. Through the years, I'd heard one side of some extremely heated phone calls my dad had had. Mostly, they consisted of some disgruntled small-business owner telling him off while he muttered things like, "I'm sorry about that," and "I understand, but Jennings purchasing the business is the best bet for survival." It was no secret that Jennings was in the business of acquiring its small-business rivals, running over the Georgia tech industry like a vacuum. I almost shivered at the thought. I hated that about it.

We speed past the resort, and the farther we go, the quieter the lake seems to get. There are less boats, less houses, and less businesses popping up on the shore. There are more trees now, and the few houses we do drive past seem to be hidden behind them, like the trees are protecting them from the madness of the water. Unlike the houses in Rich Man's Cove that seem to have cleared everything in their path so they could boast, these ones seem to be trying to camouflage themselves into the trees.

We turn down another cove, and he cuts the engine off completely. He hops up from the driver's seat and walks up to the front of the boat with me. I tuck my feet under myself to make room for him and scoot back slightly so he has room. He sits down and straightens his legs out, stretching his arms out on either side of the seat.

"See that house?" he asks with a nod of his head. I turn to look, squinting my eyes. I see it tucked back behind the trees. It's big. Not Rich-Man's-Cove big, but it's impressive. I can see a large stone patio and a hammock up in the grass behind it. It's a log house with a forest-green roof. There are balconies popping out of multiple places, and I daydream for a moment about what it would be like to wake up, open the door, and step out onto it.

"Yeah," I finally answer him. He scoots a little closer to me, and I can smell that same after-shave scent that makes my heart rate accelerate.

"It was May's," he says close to my ear. "And now, it's yours."

My lips part as I stare up at it.

"Mine," I whisper. His hand brushes against mine on the seat, and I gasp subconsciously.

"Yours." I breathe in and out slowly, staring at the beauty in front of me. "You wanna go see it?"

I whip my head to him.

"Now?"

He nods. I turn back to the house.

"Will she...will we be...alone?"

"Haven's not home," he says. "She's staying with my mom for a while."

I swallow.

"Let's do it," I say. He smiles at me and reaches a hand out to pat my bare knee. He makes his way back to the driver's seat and kicks the engine into gear again. He turns the boat toward the house and aims it for the boat slip out in front of it. He cuts the engine off and tosses the bumper back into the water on his side. As the boat nears the dock, he hops off and ties it down. He holds a hand up to me as I climb up onto the seat. I take it and reach my foot out to step onto the dock. But I miss.

I stumble off the boat and onto my knees across the wood. Before my face hits it, though, he yanks on my hand and grabs onto my other arm, pulling me up before I become a total catastrophe.

"Damn," he mutters. I want to die, but luckily, I'm a pro at making a complete fool of myself in front of people.

"Yeah, this happens a lot." I shrug. "If you're gonna be around me, you'll have to get used to it."

He looks down at me, and that corner of his full lips pulls up again, that half-smile sending a zap to my very core.

"I hope I get a chance to, then," he says. I bite my lip again, and he turns toward the house. That's when I notice he's still holding my hand. He catches me looking down at them, interlocked. "I'm not taking a chance. I'll be holding this till we get to land." He makes himself laugh as I playfully nudge his shoulder.

"I'm not *that* tragic," I tell him.

"Eh. You'll have to prove that to me."

We get to the grass, and I feel a wave of anxiety hit me. I freeze as we stare up at the house, quiet, like it's frozen in time, waiting for its rightful owner to come breathe life back into it.

"You okay?" he asks. I slowly turn to him and nod my head.

"Uh, yeah, yeah. Let's go." He looks down at me and cocks his head, like he's not sure if he can trust me.

"I'm fine, really." I take a step in front of him, and he follows quickly behind. The patio is even bigger than it looked from the water, paved in stone with a big fire pit in the middle of it. Adirondack chairs are circled around it, and a few chaise lounges sit off to the side. There's a deck that stretches off the center of the house, but the stairs are blocked off.

"May wanted the deck to extend to either end of the house," he says. "I promised her I'd get it done. I didn't get that chance while she was alive, but I'm finishing it now. It's a work in progress, so it's not usable right now."

I nod.

"You can...you can build?"

He laughs.

"I can do a lot of things," he says. "I'm pretty good with my hands."

Our eyes meet again, and I know there's some deeper meaning behind his innocent words. And the thought makes me shiver. His hands were one of the first things I noticed about him—long and dark with thick veins leading up to his bulging forearms.

"I have a key," he says, reaching into his back pocket to pull out his keychain.

"You mean we can go inside?" I ask. He dangles the key and nods. I turn back slowly to the house, staring up at the huge floor-to-ceiling windows that are plastered across it. I picture the get-togethers that happened on this patio, the people that lounged in these chairs. The crisped, dripping marshmallows that probably fell into the fire pit on occasion.

May, staring out the windows as she drank her morning coffee.

Or was it tea?

Or maybe it was neither.

And maybe none of these things happened. I wouldn't know because I missed it all. I missed her. I missed my sister. Man, that word is still so foreign to me. It was so forbidden, so taboo my whole life. And now it's being shouted at me from the top of the tallest mountain here in Meade Lake.

So many lies, so many things to learn about my own self.

And then I feel a tightness in my chest. The lump in my throat makes it harder to take in a deep breath, and I feel the stinging behind my eyes of tears that are threatening to drop any minute.

"I...I, um, I think—" I stammer. He steps in front of me, blocking the house from my view completely. He reaches down and takes my hand in his.

"Hey," he says. "We don't have to do this today. Let's get you back to your car, okay?"

Thank God. Thank God he said it so I didn't have to.

I'm not ready.

I follow Derrick back down to the dock, and when we reach it, he playfully takes my hand again.

"I'm not taking any chances," he says. I manage to crack a smile.

"If I didn't know any better, I'd say you just want to keep holding my hand." He looks down at me and gives me a curious look, his eyebrows shooting up. Then, much to my dismay, he drops my hand. Instead, he moves his hand to the small of my back and gently leads me to the boat.

He helps me on and unties us, and we each pull our bumper up. As he pulls us out, I look back at the house one more time. May's house. *My* house.

9

W e boat back to the store, and Derrick drives me back to Alma's. When we pull in, we see Haven's car still parked in the driveway. He looks at her car then turns to me.

"I'm gonna just head back to the B&B," I tell him. "Can you please tell Alma thank you again?"

He nods quietly.

"Are you sure you don't wanna—"

"Nah," I cut him off. "Not tonight. I'm not gonna ruin her day any more than I already have."

He shakes his head.

"You didn't ruin it. I did," he says. "But it's not her decision. And I know you haven't seen the best side of her yet. But she really is great. I swear." His face breaks into a smile, and I can't help but reciprocate.

"If you say so," I chuckle. I reach my hand to my handle, but he grabs my hand before I can move any further.

"I hope you'll stay for a while," he says. "Just to get to know the area. And her."

I swallow, our eyes trained on each other.

And you. I nod.

"So, for the funeral tomorrow, did you still want to come?" he asks. I swallow. *No.*

"Yes."

"Do you want me to pick you up? The family is, uh, I mean, we were all gonna go up early to be there to greet people."

I swallow. *The family.*

"No, no. I'll come separately," I say. He tilts his head.

"Kaylee, we want…you're a part of—"

"I'm not," I say, shaking my head. "I'm not. I'll just see you there, okay?"

I slip out of his truck and tuck my hair behind my ears. "Thank you for today."

I walk across the gravel and get into my car.

As I pull out of the driveway, like clockwork, my phone rings. It's my father, and just seeing his name flash on my screen makes my queasy. I've been putting off my life—or, at least, my life in Georgia—for days now. I need a plan. I hit *decline* and quickly command my car to call Charlotte.

"Char, hey," I say.

"Hi! I was just thinking about you. What's going on there? How is it?"

"It's…it's good," I say. "But listen, I need you and Emma to do something for me. I need more time here. There's a lot for me to go through. I will fill you in on it, I swear. But I need time that's uninterrupted by them. First, I need you to go to my apartment, grab some clothes, and ship them up here to me. I'll text you the address and pay you for the shipping. Second, I have a plan. Will you go along with it?"

"You know I will," she says. Like I said, world-class best friend. The kind that revs up for the plan before she even knows what it is. When I park in the driveway, I open up a text.

Hi, Dad. Sorry I didn't answer.

Where have you been? I gulp.

I took a trip.

A trip? He answers back instantly.

Yes. I need some space.

My phone rings again. I decline.

Answer your phone, he types. I don't respond.

Kaylee. Where are you? Your mother is worried now.

I pause and look out over the water again.

You can let Mom know I'm safe. I took a trip with Charlotte and Emma to Miami, I send off.

Miami? What the hell is in Miami? I sigh. I can picture his face growing red, that vein in his forehead sticking out the way it does when he feels like he's losing control.

For a few minutes, there's nothing. No text, no calls. Just as I scoot off my chair, my phone rings again. When I don't answer, he texts me again.

You have a week.

I need more time than that. I'm having a bit of a quarter-life crisis.

Silence again. It's not often that I render him speechless. But he needs me there. He could replace me, sure. With someone a lot more prepared. But that someone wouldn't have his last name. Wouldn't be the right "face" of the company—at least in my dad's eyes. He needs me.

I'll give you a month.

My heart is beating a million miles a minute. I don't often speak out toward my dad. After

all, he's pretty much given me everything I've ever wanted—and even things I *didn't* want (i.e. a major stepping stone in my professional career that I in no way earned). He likes me quiet, compliant. Like my mom.

Thanks is all I can force myself to type back.

I'M LYING in the bed in my room at the inn, staring up at the ceiling. Green ivy wallpaper is plastered across it. *Who wallpapers a ceiling?* I have the doors to the balcony open, the lake air chilly and refreshing as it seeps in. I hear frogs and bugs singing in unison out in the wild, sounds I've never heard lying in any bed in Georgia.

I sit up to grab my pajamas from my bag when I hear something hit the floor. It's the gargantuan file that Alma and Jeffrey gave me. I take in a deep breath as I bend down to pick it up. I plop back down on the bed and open it up. I scan through the files, reading over May's wishes again. It's a strange thing, knowing how much thought she put into me when I didn't know enough about her to formulate a single one.

I flip through the pages, freezing again when I see the sum of May's assets—my half. A half that could sit me on Rich Man's Cove if I wanted. I shake my head and keep flipping. I stop again when I read Haven's name.

Haven Rae Dean. Dean. There's something that strikes me—envy, maybe—about Haven having May's last name. But then again, who else's would she have? She doesn't know her father, and she *certainly* wouldn't have my father's. I shake my head again.

I have a *sister.* A living, breathing sister who currently wishes *I* was the one who didn't exist. But a sister, nonetheless. And one day, if she can ever stand the sight of me, I have some questions I want to ask her.

I flip to the next file, and I realize it's the placeholder for the ledger Jeffrey mentioned would be coming, the one that outlined May's investment plan into the local businesses. After my tour with Derrick yesterday, I find myself a little more anxious to see which businesses I might recognize. And I wonder how much cloudier that will make things for me. I close my eyes and lean back, trying to clear up the fog that's falling around me.

I'm standing on the edge of some sort of water, although, it doesn't look like Meade Lake. The water is so dark it's almost black, and heavy waves crash at my feet. To my side, a woman sits in a chair facing the water, her back to me. I call to her, but she never turns around. She just stares, watching as the water comes and goes, pulling anything in its path back into its grasp and never returning it.

My eyes open, fluttering as my brain decides what's real and what was a dream. I sit up slowly, remembering what day it is: the funeral. I stand up and stretch, walking over to the sink in the corner of the room. I splash water on my face and comb my hair out then walk to my suitcase.

Fuck.

When I packed for the trip—which I originally thought was just a one-night stay at Charlotte's—funeral attire was not on my packing list.

I reach across the bed and grab my phone from the nightstand.

"Hello?" Derrick's normally cheery voice has a little edge to it today.

"Derrick, hey," I say, "sorry to bother you. I know you're probably busy this morning."

"You're good, girl. Don't apologize," he says. "Everything okay? You good?"

"Uh, yeah. I sort of forgot that I have nothing to wear today. Any place that would be open where I can grab a dress?"

There's a pause on the other end, and I hear him click his teeth.

"Man, I didn't even think of this. There's Misty's Boutique up near Timberland, but it's closed today. Pretty much everything is. Everyone is coming to the funeral."

"Shit," I mutter.

"Lemme think," he says. I pause and let him. "You know, you, uh…you and Haven are probably about the same size, don't you—"

"No," I cut him off. "No way in hell. But you did give me an idea. What about Mila?"

"Yeah, yeah, good call. Let me shoot you her number."

"Great! Thank you."

"You sure you don't wanna come with us? I can come pick you up."

The idea of being with him, arriving with him, gives my body this sort of tingle. Just to be associated with him up here gives me this feeling of security that I know I otherwise wouldn't have.

But then, the idea of others giving their condolences, seeing me, whispering. The look of utter disgust on Haven's face the two times we've met. These are all things that are not worth me living out this fantasy of being with Derrick today.

"No, no. I'm good, really," I tell him. "I'll see you there." *From the way back, where I'll be hiding.*

"I don't want you to feel like you're not...like you're not a part of this—"

"No, I got it. Thank you, Derrick. For everything."

I text Mila and explain my dilemma. She tells me she'll be by in a few with some options, and I thank her profusely and get in a quick shower. As I'm towel-drying my hair, I move my shit off the counter, and as I do, something drops out of the file from Jeffrey. I bend down to pick it up, and when I do, I see that it's an envelope addressed to me. My name is handwritten on the front in the most beautiful script I've ever seen. My hand shakes as I look down at it, because I know who it's from.

It's from May.

And just as I slip my finger in the crease, there's a knock on my door that makes me jump.

I stick it back in the file and open the door.

"Hey," Mila says, breathless from walking up the big, winding staircase in the inn.

"Oh, thank you so much for coming," I gasp, ushering her in. She lays a huge pile of dresses down on the bed and plops down next to them.

"Oh, it's no problem. Glad I could help," she says. She's all made up, her long brown hair tied back into a twisty bun-type thing. Her makeup is impeccable, and I can't help but notice how much of a knock-out she is. Something I've never been able to quite live up to, no matter how much my parents paid for pageants as a teen.

"If you need to go get Ryder and Annabelle, I can just get these back to you later," I offer, but she shakes her head.

"No, no. They're catching a ride with our friend Luna. I will be your escort today," she says, reclining back and making herself comfortable. I look at her and cock my head. "Nobody should show up to their own grandmother's funeral alone. Whether they knew her or not."

I force a smile.

"Thank you," I say just above a whisper. I pull out three dresses from the pile and slip into the bathroom to try them on. They're a little tight around the midsection, but if I suck in a bit, they work. I choose a high-necked black dress she brought, and some matching black sandals she brought with them.

"Need some help with makeup?" she asks, holding up a small pink bag. I laugh.

"That would be great. I didn't, uh, bring much of that, either," I tell her. I sit on the bed as she digs through the bag, pulling out some mascara and eyeliner and a little blush. I close my eyes and let her go.

"You feel okay about going today?" she asks me after a moment.

"Uh, yeah, I guess so," I admit. "It feels a little weird, honestly."

"Yeah, I'm sure. I can't even imagine," she tells me. "Derrick was real worried about you going alone."

I open my eyes and look at her.

"He was?" I ask. She smiles.

"Yeah. He mentioned it last night, so he was happy when I called him on the way here and told him I was picking you up. He's sort of taken a, uh, protector role toward you, I think." I swallow.

"He's been great. Sorta feels like he's the only one who's happy I'm here," I say. I'm not sure what it is about Mila that makes me feel like I can be candid with her. Maybe it's that she's not from here. She's not a Meade Lake Original, either. She had a history, a life, before this place.

"No, no," Mila says. "That's not true. Not at all. Alma, and us, we're all happy you came."

"Well, that's good to hear," I chuckle. "I don't think, uh, Haven could say the same." Mila's eyes drop to the ground.

"I just wish May could have met you. She really was an incredible woman. She changed Ryder's life."

I look up at her.

"Because of the store?"

She nods.

"Without that grant, that store never would have gotten off the ground. When Ryder went through treatment, it was our source of income. It kept us going, and—" She pauses when she sees me staring. "Uh, we haven't told you about the last year, yet, have we?"

I shake my head. She smiles.

"We'll save that for another day. But just know that May was truly one of a kind."

"So I've been told," I say. "To tell the truth, I'm a little envious of all of you, that you had that time with her."

Mila lifts her eyes to me.

"Ya know, Kaylee," she says, her voice soft as she puts her hand on my shoulder, "I think, maybe, that's how Haven feels toward you. About your mother."

My eyes grow wide, her words hitting me right in the gut. She drops her hand and walks toward the door, opening it and holding it for me.

Haven has been so cold, so unwelcoming toward me since I've been here that I

admittedly haven't given much thought to all she's missed out on. How much I had that she didn't.

The car ride to the funeral is quicker than I'm ready for, but like every other trip I've taken since I got to Meade Lake, the views make you forget just what time really means. We make a sharp turn up a steep hill, and as we drive, I realize we're headed up a mountain. Mila pulls her car into an open field once we reach the top and puts the car in park.

"Where are we?" I ask her.

"May wasn't the most religious," she tells me as she smooths her dress out. "But she was sort of spiritual in another sense. This was her favorite place in Meade Lake, on the top of this mountain." I nod as I follow her down a dirt path. We round a patch of trees toward a clearing, and that's when I see the mass of people. There has to be two hundred people here, all gathered and talking, and suddenly, I feel completely over-whelmed. Chairs are set up in rows, and a man in a black shirt and slacks walks toward the front of the group and steps up to a microphone. I look around at all the faces, wondering how one person could have made such an impact on so many.

Realizing how much of my own family, my own life, I didn't—and will never—know. I see Alma near the front row, greeting people and accepting hugs galore. Derrick is next to her, doing the same.

"Mama!" a little voice shrieks from behind us as

Annabelle runs down the path toward us. Mila scoops her up and kisses her cheek. Ryder follows close behind on the arm of a woman with long black hair.

"Hi, babe," Mila says, reaching for Ryder's hand and pulling him in for a quick kiss.

"You look great," he tells her as he draws her near. She smiles.

"You can't see," she says. He smiles back.

"Shapes and colors, my love, and that's all I need to tell you're a damn knockout." She giggles and playfully swats at his chest. "Kaylee, it's good to see you again. This is Luna, a dear friend of ours."

I smile and shake her hand.

"Kaylee, it's so nice to meet you," she says. "And I'm so sorry for your loss," she nervously adds. I smile and thank her.

"Should we head up?" Mila asks. They all start moving, but I stay frozen. Mila pauses and turns back to me.

"Please, go," I tell her, pushing my hands. "Please. I'm just going to hang back." She pauses for a moment then nods, and I'm thankful she understands me.

As the rest of the crowd takes their seats, I scan the crowd.

"This has to be weird for you," a voice says from behind me, making me jump.

"Oh, h-hi," I say. Haven is dressed in a slick black dress, her curls pulled back into a clip. Her eyes are trained on the crowd in front of us as she steps up so we're next to each other. "Yeah, it's a little strange."

"That's what happens when you don't know someone," she says. Then she slowly turns to me. "You shouldn't have come." Our eyes meet, and I freeze.

I want to say something, but my brain can't formulate the right words. Because although her words cut like a knife, the expression on her face is more than that. It's pain, total anguish. Anguish that only someone who really loved someone can feel. She draws in a breath and walks forward, making her way down the aisle and taking her seat in the front row. Derrick stands at the front, scanning the crowd. Our eyes meet, and his eyebrows jump. He takes a step in my direction, but I hold my hands up, letting him know not to tend to me. Not now. This day isn't about me. It can't be. I don't think I could handle it.

He nods and takes a seat between Alma and Haven, but through the service, I catch him turning back to me, checking to make sure I'm still there. I listen to person after person, stranger after stranger, talk about my dead grandmother with such warmth and familiarity, and I think about how strange it is that her own daughter isn't here. Her *family*.

I listen as they speak of her, intimate stories, tales of soups she made them, money she lent them, hugs she gave.

But as they speak, I feel nothing. Like I'm watching a funeral service for a complete stranger, because that's exactly what I'm doing. I turn slowly and walk back to the path, needing air. I find a tree stump and take a seat.

"You okay, girl?" I hear him ask, and I fight a smile. *Protector*.

"Hey, I'm good!" I say, trying to sound much more enthused than I feel. "Please, go back. I don't want you to miss this. For May."

He nudges me over with his hip, and I slide a bit to my right.

84

"This is exactly where May would want me to be," he says as he sits down next to me. Seeing him up close in a suit isn't exactly the most conducive for appropriate funeral thoughts, but my god, the man is stunning. "You wanna get out of here?"

I turn my head to him so quickly that it makes him chuckle.

"I'll take that as a yes," he says, popping up and offering me his hand.

"Are you sure? I don't want you to feel like you have to leave because of me."

He doesn't say anything, just holds his hand out. I look down at it then back up at him before slipping mine into his.

10

"This is the only place in town still open today, I think," he says as he reaches through the window of the snow cone shop and grabs two for us. I thank him and grab mine, and we walk down off the pier and onto the grass. Mila's shoes don't quite fit me right, so I slip them off and hook my fingers through them. The grass feels good between my toes, and I feel the tense anxiety I was feeling on top of that mountain slowly slipping away. He leads me down the grass close to the water and points to the ground.

"This okay?" he asks. I nod and sit down as gracefully as possible, smoothing the dress down and tucking my legs underneath me.

"So, doing okay? I'm sure you were feeling a lot of things up there."

I take a bite of the blue ice and let it slide down my throat.

"Honestly...I think I was so anxious because I felt like I wasn't feeling *enough.*" I can feel the words coming out, like I have no control over what I say in front of him. "I looked around at all of you up there today, listening to story after story about a woman who wasn't even so much as a memory to me. She's someone I barely remember, and even after she was gone, she was someone I was taught never to speak of. How can I mourn someone like that?"

He takes a thoughtful bite of his cone.

"You can't," he says matter-of-factly. "It breaks my heart, though, that you missed out on each other. Everyone should have gotten to meet May."

I nod and offer an extremely forced smile.

"Look, I know you've got a lot to think about right now, but if you stick around for a bit, I'd love to show you around. There are so many people here that can tell you stories about her, make you feel like...like you knew her, almost. If you want to, I mean."

I look at him, and my breath catches. The sun is reflecting off the water in front of us and shining into his eyes, leaving glints of gold and orange in the bright brown.

"I'd like that," I tell him. "I'm...I'm still processing everything. May not really being dead, then *actually* being dead, the money, the house. Haven. But I do want to get to know more about her. Everything I missed." I swallow and scoot the tiniest bit closer to him. "It wouldn't be the most terrible thing to get to know you a little bit more, either."

A smile tugs at the corner of his mouth, exposing a set of teeth fit for a damn toothpaste ad. He leans back on his arm, nudging it behind me, and I feel my heart rate accelerate. He looks down at me and bites his bottom lip gently, sending a shock through my core that seems to pool right between my legs. But just as quick as he cages me in, he scoots away, sending my libido nose-diving to the bottom of the lake. He clears his throat and dusts his lap off then pulls himself onto his feet, and I feel a wave of embarrassment. I can't read him. And maybe it's because I've been out of the game too long, and I can't tell what's a move and what's not. He's friendly and concerned about me, and he's approached flirting on more than one occasion. But more than once now, it's like he remembers something. Or maybe some*one?* Maybe I've been naive enough to think he's that delectable and is still an eligible bachelor. Or maybe there's something else going on. But whatever the reason, there's some sort of barrier he builds between us whenever he seems to realize his guard is down. He reaches a hand out to me, and I hesitate for a moment.

"So, listen, the repast is at May's house," he says. "I know you weren't quite ready to go there yesterday."

Listening to those stories, feeling so distant from May, makes me wonder if I need to make a move to *feel* closer. To feel *her.*

"I'm ready today," I tell him. He tilts his head to the side.

"You sure? No one will be there for a while. We can go, and I can give you the tour before people get there, if you want to see it before it's loaded with people." I smile and nod and follow him back to his truck. I pay attention as he drives, slowly trying to learn my way around the town, which general direction the few acquaintances I've met here live. I've only seen May's house by boat, though, so this is all new territory.

We drive down Lakeshore Highway, past what I recognize to be the road that leads to Alma's. We keep driving, past Big Moon Sports, then past Lou's. Finally, he veers off the road to the left, down another long, winding, wooded road. As we drive, the houses grow more scarce, and the trees take over. The lake follows us through the trees as if it's guiding us. Then, he makes one final left turn down a gravel driveway, and I see it in all its wooden magnificence. It's immaculate, the landscaping pristine enough to be on the front cover of a magazine. Two rocking chairs sit perched on the front porch, and the house seems to be plastered with huge windows. It's just as beautiful on this side as it was from the water. He's at my door before I can pick my jaw up off the ground and helps me out.

"So, this is it," he says. He plucks a key from his keychain and leads me up the steps to the front door. When he opens it, I'm hit with the smell of pine. We step into a grand foyer, and I follow him into the great room behind it. Floor-to-ceiling windows let in loads of natural light. There's a massive island topped in granite to my left in the chef's kitchen, and doors that lead out to a deck off the great room. A large staircase sits in the corner of the room, and it *had* to be professionally decorated. Beautiful paintings hang on every wall. I twirl around, taking in every corner, every knot in the wood floors, every bit of light that seeps in to warm us up.

"Wow," I whisper.

"Yeah," he says. "So, this is where May made her famous Bolognese sauce." We walk toward the kitchen as he holds his arms out. "This is the table where she kicked my ass in poker on more than one occasion." I laugh out loud. I follow him around to every end of the house, still ogling at the beauty of this house.

"Up here," he says as he takes the stairs two-by-two, "are the other bedrooms. There are a few in the basement, too. This," he says, pushing open one of the thick pine doors, "is Haven's room." I look around, and I suddenly feel a bit like I'm intruding. I can't help but notice, though, that her bedspread is made of teals and greens—my favorite colors. And on the small desk in the corner of the room sits a vase of sunflowers. My favorite flower.

I follow him down to the other end of the hall. He takes a breath as he pushes open one of the doors.

"This was May's room," he says. I look around, more light spilling into the massive suite from the windows and sliding glass doors. But he doesn't move to step inside the room, and neither do I. He closes the door slowly and blows out another breath. Then he walks me to the last door at the end of the hall. "And this," he says, pushing the door open ever so slowly, "was yours, if you ever wanted it."

I look at him, my lips parting a bit.

The room isn't near as big as May's, but it's the stuff of dreams. A bench in the bay window to my left and big sliding doors that lead to a private balcony at the back of it. He nods his head as if to let me know it's okay for me to explore it. And I do. I step inside, noticing every single detail. The wooden logs that make up the walls, the softness of the carpets. The pine furniture that matches the rest of the house. The beautiful handmade quilt that's draped across the bed. I walk toward the balcony doors and flick the lock open.

I step outside and look out over the water. I close my eyes as a breeze rushes through, blowing my hair back and sending a shiver down my spine.

"Amazing," is all I can muster up as my eyes drink in everything around me. Before I realize it, he's next to me. He looks down to me, towering over me like the trees around us.

"It is," he says, his eyes piercing into mine. I tuck a strand of hair behind my ear.

"I can't believe, after all this time, she waited for me," I whisper. I jump slightly when I feel his hand brush up against mine on the railing.

"She must have known you were worth waiting for," he says. Our eyes meet again for the briefest moment before he jumps back and clears his throat, walking back through the door.

Just as we're making our way down the steps, we hear the front door open. He turns back to me as I step onto the last step.

"It's gonna get crazy here today," he tells me. "If you need to go, if you need *me*, find me."

I nod slowly, my stomach flipping again. *God, why does this keep happening?*

Alma walks through the front door, carrying an armful of platters, bags draped on either arm. I scurry to help her while Derrick goes out to her car to get more. Haven follows closely behind, carrying a stack of casserole dishes in her arms, but she barely looks at any of us as she walks them to the kitchen and puts them on the island. Alma starts giving us instructions on things to heat up, stir, and dish out, and as Derrick and I shuffle around the kitchen, I notice Haven walking up the steps, then I hear a bedroom door open and shut shortly after.

"That girl will never be the same after this," Alma says over my shoulder, eyeing the stairs.

11

I'm able to keep myself busy, helping unwrap all the dishes people are bringing in, filling up the ice buckets, and stirring whatever is simmering on the stove. I'm not usually so introverted; I actually thrive in situations where I have to be loud, make my presence known. It's something I got from my dad, I guess, whether I wanted it or not.

"Let people know you're there. That's how you get the big office, kid."

All his little tidbits of "wisdom" he passed on to me throughout the years seem so tainted now.

Right now, though, I'm more comfortable fading into the background. Not because I don't know the people around me; I don't have a problem breaking the ice. It's more that I don't feel like I know my*self.* Like all these people around me know more about my family history than I do.

"Sweetie, put that spoon down and come on outside. There are a lot of people out here who want to meet you," Alma says from behind me. I sigh. So much for blending in. I wipe my hands on the kitchen towel and brush my hair back off my shoulder. She puts her arm around me as she walks me outside, and I feel at ease the moment she touches me.

"Everyone, this is Kaylee!" Alma all but shouts as we walk onto the deck. I'm met with cheers and "hellos" from every angle. I turn and wave to them all simultaneously, trying to remember their faces and names as she guides me to the table.

"This is Abby," Alma says, pointing to a middle-aged woman at the corner of the deck, sipping lemonade. "She and her family own Shirley's Diner up toward the edge of town. That's her husband, Rick, down there."

"It's so nice to meet you, Kaylee," Abby says. "We've all heard so much about you."

Can't say the same.

"Thank you, it's so nice to meet you, too," I say with my best forced smile.

"And this is Luna, I think you met her," Alma says. Luna and I nod to each other, and I'm thankful for a familiar face. "That's Patsy and Pete, they live right up the street here. That's Darby there, another good friend of May's. I think you met my other son, Teddy." Teddy nods in my direction, and I wave back. "And you met my grandbabies. And you know Mila and Ryder." Mila winks at me, and I like that I already have someone who feels like a friend here. Or, at least, a friend that I don't picture naked all the time, like I do with Derrick. It's *very* distracting.

"And we know she knows Derrick," Teddy says with a mischievous laugh, and I swallow and look around. Not everyone seems to be clued in to Teddy's joke, thankfully, but Alma pinches his arm as he walks by.

Derrick catches my eyes from below the deck, narrowing his eyes at me and showing off that perfect smile. *Ugh.* I shouldn't be lusting after someone so hard at a damn *funeral.* My *grandmother's* funeral, to be specific.

Yep. I'm going straight to hell.

"And *this,*" Alma says, making me stand at attention. I didn't realize the introductions were still going on. "This right here is Lou Baker. You've probably seen his grill up on the highway."

"Ah, yes. Derrick showed me on our tour. So, you're *that* Lou, huh?" I ask. Alma motions to the chair next to Lou, and I smile and take it.

"Honey, I'm the *only* Lou that's worth knowing." He smiles, and I can't help but smile back immediately. He's got a few caps on his teeth and long, white hair that's pulled back into a ponytail that points down his back. The sleeves of his dress shirt are rolled up, and his forearms are loaded with faded tattoos that look like they might have been done with the tip of a pen thirty or forty years ago. "It's so nice to meet you."

"It's nice to meet you, too, Lou," I tell him, and I mean it.

"Your grandmother was an angel on this earth," he says, and echoes of "here, here" pop up around the table. "And there are quite a few of us here today who wouldn't be without her."

His eyes are a vibrant blue, and they drop to his hands on the table. "Me included."

I narrow my eyes at him. He leans back in his chair and shimmies his suit jacket off, draping it on his chair. The air is cool for it being the end of summer, but it's warm enough to make you sweat in a full suit.

"When I first got to Meade Lake about fifteen years

ago, I was a damn mess. Ain't that so, Alma?" He looks up at her, grabbing her forearm. She pats his hand and kneels down to kiss his forehead.

"You know I love you, Lou. But you were a *mess,*" she says, and they share a chuckle.

"I'd been using drugs for twenty years before that. Lost my wife, lost custody of my kid, lost my job. Lost everything. And never got any of that back. Not even my kid."

My heart sinks in my chest.

"I came here to stay with a friend of mine until I could get back on my feet. But the problem was, I wasn't ready to get on my feet. So, I drank and did more drugs for about a year. Got arrested a number of times, spent a few nights in jail. Till finally, my friend gave up on me, too. Told me he couldn't handle it. And I can't say I blame him. So, there I was, walking down Lakeshore Highway with everything I owned in a damn backpack, in my forties, and homeless. What a chump I was."

Alma rubs his shoulder as he goes on.

"A car pulls up to me, whistles out the window, then pulls over in front of me. And who hops out? The most beautiful woman I'd ever seen. She walked up to me and looked me dead in the eyes. Told me her name was May, and she'd seen me walking around aimlessly and had seen me asleep on a few public benches and in the back of restaurants on occasion. Asked me what I wanted if I could have anything. Be anything. I told her *a father* first. Then, I'd want to own my own restaurant.

"She thought for a moment then told me she'd make me a deal. Told me if I got into a rehab facility and got clean, she'd lend me money to lease out this old building on the side of the highway. She'd help me start a restaurant. Then, she told me maybe, one day, I'd get the chance to be a father again. I'm still waiting for that." He pauses as a pained smile crosses his lips.

"But I did it. I checked into rehab for two months. She lent me money to rent a small apartment about a mile from the grille. Then, she took me to the leasing office, and we signed all the paperwork. And Lou's Lakeside Grille was born. And so was the new Lou."

I nod slowly as I take it all in.

"That's amazing, Lou," I mutter. He nods.

"Sweetie, *she* was amazing. One of my dearest friends. Just like Alma, here." He kisses her hand, and she pats him again.

"There are a lot of us here who can tell you stories like that, Kaylee," Abby says. "May changed us all. Taught us to care about each other. She was like family."

"Yeah," someone echoes.

"Amen," Alma says next to me.

"She *was* family." All heads whip in the direction of the back door where Haven stands, her arms wrapped around herself. Lou stands and wraps her in a hug, and everyone grows quiet. I can hear her stifled sobs on his chest, and I look away. It seems like tears are falling from everyone's eyes, except for mine. I slowly stand up and excuse myself from the table and walk back inside. I put my hands on the cool granite counter, wondering how—*what* the hell I'm supposed to feel. But while I figure it out, I know I need a break. I reach for my purse that's tucked underneath the island and pull my keys from it. And then I remember that I don't have a car here.

"I'm sorry, sweetheart," I hear Alma say as she walks

in and stands next to me. "I know she was a stranger to you."

I nod.

"But maybe being here, meeting all of us… Maybe that will give you some indication of the kind of woman she was. *Who* she was," she says. I nod again. "So, what do you think of the house?"

I look up at the cathedral ceilings, the giant log rafters that stretch across it from corner to corner.

"It's gorgeous," I tell her. "It's strange. I felt sort of… calm today, when I first stepped inside." She smiles.

"May'll do that to ya," she says. "Listen, Haven is staying with me for a while. She doesn't want to be alone, not that I blame her. If you want to check out of the inn, you can stay here. This is *your* house."

My eyes meet hers, and I smile. I nod.

"I think I'd like that."

"Good." She walks toward a hook on the wall and pulls off a key. "This is the key to May's Explorer out there. It's probably as old as you, but Derrick kept it running good. It's yours. Why don't you go get your things and come back? Some people will have left, and it'll be a little quieter. We'll be out of your hair soon."

I smile.

"I don't mind," I tell her, but I'm lying a little. It'll be nice to get my bearings here in this house alone. I thank her and walk toward the door, but then I freeze. "Alma, can you tell Derrick I said goodbye?" I ask. She smiles.

"Of course, baby," she says. I smile, and as I reach for the door, I turn back.

"And Haven?"

She freezes, her expression growing more serious.

"Of course."

. . .

WHEN I GET BACK to the inn, I throw the few things I actually have in my bag and tidy up a bit. I make my way down the steps to the front desk, bag in hand. But when I get there, Mrs. Miller pops up from behind the desk, her eyebrows shooting up.

"Leaving so soon?" she asks, and I can hear the fear in her voice. I remember what Mila told me.

Ever since the Willington Ski Resort opened a few years back, the rest of the inns around here have had some trouble filling up.

"No, not just yet. Just going to stay at a friend's tonight. But I'm not checking out yet, if that's okay with you," I tell her. I watch her shoulder shrink in relief. After all, I'm a manager now. Oh yeah, and a millionaire. I can afford to pay for a few extra nights at this inn, even if I don't stay.

"Oh, great. We'll see you soon, sweetie!" she calls behind me as I walk back out to the parking lot. I realize now that I have two cars parked in the lot: mine and May's Explorer. As I look at the shiny, brand-spanking-new car my dad had surprised me with a few months earlier, I feel disgust. I recognize it was just another ploy, another pawn for his control. I opt for the Explorer, get in, and head toward May's house. Toward *my* house.

When I pull up, the only car left is Alma's.

"There you are," she says, putting the last of the platters away in the cabinet above the stove.

"I'm sorry," I tell her. "I missed cleaning up."

"Don't worry about it, baby," she says, waving me off. "We're all good here. Get all your things?" I nod and hold my bag up. I look around the kitchen and into the great room.

"He's not here," she says, wiping down the counters.

"Huh? Who?" I ask, feigning innocence. Her lips curve up into a smile as one of her eyebrows shoot up.

"My boy," she says, putting her hand on her hip. "He took Haven back to my house for the night. She'd had enough."

I could deny that I was looking for him, but I don't really see the use in it.

"How was she?"

Alma shrinks.

"She just lost the person who her whole world revolved around, baby," she says. "Not good. That type of hole in your heart never does heal."

I nod and look down at the ground. She folds the towel over the rack on the front of the oven then turns to me.

"Okay, baby. Everything should be in order. All the leftovers from today are in the fridge in case you get hungry. Need me to show you around?" she asks.

"I think I got it," I tell her. "Thank you, Alma."

"Always, baby. You don't know it yet, but you're family now." When she smiles at me, I see just how much Derrick looks like her. I nod, and we say our good-byes. And then the exhaustion hits. I lock the front door and trudge up the big staircase, looking out over the railing through the gigantic windows. I can see the moonlight sprinkled across the water, trailing up to the trees. It's breathtaking.

My room is just as clean and tidy as it was this morning when I first saw it, and I can't believe it's *mine*. I slip my shoes off and throw my bag on the bed. When I do, the files from Jeffrey slide out, and I see the corner of the envelope sticking out. I swallow and tug it out.

I sit on the bed and take a breath before slipping my finger into the seam and tearing it open.

DEAR KAYLEE,

THERE'S SO MUCH I want to say to you, but none of it will change the fact that we lost so much time together. I was faced with a choice, and it was one I hope you'll never have to make. I hope hearts change and time heals. But if it doesn't, then maybe you'll understand why I made the choice I made.

I don't want to waste words on your mother and father; I won't berate them and tell you how I feel about them. My decision to come here and leave Georgia was never about them. It was about her. I made the decision to stay in Haven's life, to be her family when she had none. I made the decision to raise her and let her know how much she was loved. And I've never regretted it; I've never doubted that it was the right decision.

The only thing I regret is that choosing to raise her meant having to give up all contact with you. It meant not knowing who you'd grow into, not knowing if your favorite color would change. Not knowing if you'd still look like me. It meant not being there for birthdays, graduations. But I kept my hope that one day I'd find you.

One day, one of those letters I'd sent, one of those calls would get through to you. I'm sorry they didn't. I'm sorry they never made it to you. But know that I sent them, Kaylee. Know that every day, I said a prayer for you. I wanted you to be happy. I still do.

I needed to make sure your sister knew she was loved, just like you were. I needed her to know that her existence was not a shame, but a blessing. And it is, Kaylee. She's the most wonderful human, much like I imagine you are. We didn't know each other in life,

Kaylee. But I'll be there, watching you after it. If you spend time here at the water, I know you'll find yourself loving her the way I did.

Kaylee, no matter what life you choose, know that I love you. I'm proud of you.

I'll SEE you in the next life, my sweet Kaylee.

ALL MY LOVE,

Gran May

I FOLD the letter back up, my hands shaking, and everything is suddenly thick and heavy around me. The stories from Lou and Alma, Haven's face, her sobs. The tears of complete strangers.

My own memories of that day at the hospital. Her disappearing through those hospital doors and never coming back to me.

My mother, who braided my hair for every dance recital. My father who cheered me on at every race I ever ran. Both of them, who sat front and center at my high school and college graduations. Who only ever wanted the best for me. Who wanted me to *be* the best. Who wanted me to carry on their name, their traditions, their business.

We choose family.

But they didn't. My mother did *not* choose her family. She chose marriage, and status, and money. She chose the life she had over the life she made. She chose *me*. But she didn't choose Haven.

As I stare down at the folded page in my hands, a tear lands on it. Then another, then another. And I can't stop them. I reach up to touch them as they stream down my face. *This* is the pain they were all feeling today. This is a glimpse into what life was like with May, and what it will be without her.

I walk across the room and open the sliding glass door. I step out onto the balcony in my bare feet. Up here, I'm as high as some of the trees, and the moon is so bright it feels like there's a spotlight on me. I sit down on the bench that's perched in the corner of the balcony and stare up at it, not bothering to dry the tears anymore. I let them fall, seeping into my skin, just as her words have.

I'll see you in my next life.

12

———

Eeeeeeeeerrrrrrrrrrrrreeeerrrrrrr.

I jump up to the roaring of some sort of machine coming to life beneath me, and when I do, my first thought is pain. I fell asleep on the balcony, and I'm feeling it. My neck is twisted and stiff, and my skin is sticky from the outside air. I look down over the railing, trying to figure out where the noise is coming from.

Derrick steps out from underneath the deck, a pencil in his mouth and the culprit in his hand: a blaring chainsaw. He has his back to me as he walks toward a plank of wood he has set up in the yard, then he starts to saw. I watch him for a few moments, soaking in his every move. I need to get a closer look.

I walk back inside and down the stairs, peering out at him from the giant windows in the great room. I unlock the back door slowly and step out onto the deck as slowly and stealthily as possible. I'm not ready to be seen yet. I just want to *do* the seeing.

Then something magical happens.

Derrick turns around with the sawed-off plank in hand, and as he does, a gust of wind blows. The whole world spins in slow motion as the breeze blows his unbuttoned shirt out from his body, exposing the most perfect chest-and-ab combo I have ever seen with my own two eyes. Not even the jagged scar on the right side of his chest affects its perfection.

With every step he takes, muscles bulge from his arms, his shoulders, his stomach, like some sort of topographic map that my eyes are following like a lost dog. He reaches his free hand up to wipe his brow, and that's when he looks up. I try to duck down, but I trip over a plank that's sticking up and go flying backward on my ass. On my way down, I reach for something—*anything*—to catch my fall, but lucky me, the only thing in grabbing distance is a small potted plant. The plant crashes to the ground, the pot shattering.

I cover my face with my hands and surrender to the embarrassment. There's not a chance he didn't see it. And even if he didn't, there's no *way* he didn't hear it.

Before I can recover, he's bursting through the back door of the house.

"Girl, what are you *doing?*" he asks before bending down to assess the damage. He's looking at all my limbs to make sure I'm not badly hurt, and while he does, I'm staring at him. Every inch of his skin that I can see. I'm drinking it in. It's better than I've been imagining. *Way* better. "You good? You hurt anywhere?"

I shake my head.

"Nope. I would say I bruised my ego, but I'm so used to this by now that it doesn't even phase me," I tell him. He laughs as he hooks his arms under mine and pulls me to my feet. The early morning sun is making those speckles in his eyes again. He catches me eyeing him, and he bites his bottom lip to keep from smiling.

"What are you doing here?" he asks just as he reaches up to wipe a smudge of dirt off my forehead from the plant.

"Thanks," I tell him. "I, uh, I'm staying here now. Alma's idea."

He nods.

"Man, sorry about that. Mama didn't mention you were doing that just yet. I was trying to get this deck done for ya. I wouldn't have started so early, had I known."

I wave him off.

"No problem. I get up early to run usually, anyway," I tell him as I turn back toward the door. He follows me back inside.

"You run?" he asks.

"Try to, every day. I haven't since I've been up here, though. It's throwing me off."

"Want some company?" My breathing picks up at the very thought.

"You run?" I ask.

"Try to, every day," he says with a wink. Not that him doing anything physical is unbelievable, judging by his body.

"Then, yeah, that'd be great. You can show me the good routes," I tell him, bending down to grab my shoes. When I stand up, I catch his eyes on my ass, and then they meet mine. But he doesn't look away in shame; he looks right at me. Right into my eyes, letting me know. I bite my lip in response.

"You're in the mountains now, girl," he says,

brushing past me. "All routes are good. I'll meet you out front."

I run upstairs and throw on a pair of shorts and a tank top. I lace my shoes up and head out the front door, locking it behind me and tying the key to my shoelaces. When I get out there, he's sitting on the porch step in nothing but basketball shorts and his shoes. He pops up when he hears me, and my eyes go right to his body again. He looks at me.

"Do you mind?" he asks, motioning to his body.

"Oh, no, no problem," I tell him. Then my eyes catch his, and I feel that heat wave wash over me. I grab for the hem of my tank top and pull it up over my head, dropping it in a ball on the porch. His eyes widen as he scans my body, my hot-pink sports bra bright in the morning sun. "Do you?"

He bites his bottom lip.

"Not at all," he says. We walk to the end of the driveway and turn left down the street. "How long you wanna go today?"

I feel my competitive nature kick in. It's been a few days since I've run, but I don't back down. Ever.

"As long as you want to," I tell him. He smiles as he starts to jog, me following his lead.

"Well, I'd love to take you on my favorite route," he says, "but we're in the mountains now, girl. You sure you're up for it?"

I shoot him a look.

"Let's do it," I tell him. He nods, and we pick up the pace a little bit. As we get out on the main road, I drop behind him so we're in single file, but I make sure to keep right on his heels. I want him to hear my breath, feel the heat from my body. I want him to know I'm close.

"We're gonna cross the street up here in a minute," he tells me over his shoulder. I follow him across the street once we have a clearance, and he heads toward the start of a path. He pauses for a minute and turns to me. "You ready for this?"

I shoot him a look and put my hands on my hips.

"Are *you?*" I ask before taking off past him onto the dirt trail. It takes me all of three strides to realize that this trail is an incline—one that doesn't appear to plateau anytime soon. In front of me, all I can see is trees and trail, and everything is pointed up. *Fuck.* We're literally running up a damn mountain, and now that I've established myself as some sort of ultra-runner, I have to keep this up. I hear him on my heels, his breathing low and steady. My body reacts involuntarily, my feet picking up the pace as every muscle in my legs screams at me to slow down. My quads and my ass are tensing up, and my lungs are on fire, but I can't let up. He pushes up next to me so we're shoulder to shoulder, and I'm not sure what we'll do if we come across someone coming from the other direction. There is absolutely no more room on this trail.

"Need to slow down?" he asks from next to me, and I can hear the smug smile in his voice. "We got about a quarter mile left."

"That ain't nothin'," I say, trying like hell not to let him hear how out of breath I am. I pride myself on being in good shape. I run almost every day; I eat fairly healthy. But I might not be in mountain-running shape. And judging by his physique, he's no stranger to working out, either.

I push further, pretty sure I'm going to pass out. The scenery around us is enough to take my breath away—if I had any breath left, of course. Trees surround us, everything shades of green. We hop over roots, step on rocks, and duck under low-hanging branches, our strides completely in sync. To my relief, his breathing is quickening now, too. He lifts a finger up ahead to a clearing in the trees, and I can see the sky.

"That's it," he pants, and I breathe out a long breath of relief. We push a little bit harder, a little bit faster, up one more steep incline, and then we make it to the edge of the trees, the end of the trail, and we're in a wide-open field. We run through the edge of the forest like it's a finish line then hunch over to catch our breath.

"Damn, girl," he says with a smile as he wipes his brow on his forearm. "I wasn't expecting a full-on race today."

I chuckle as I gulp in the mountain air, catching a drop of sweat on the strap of my sports bra.

"What were you expecting?" I ask him. He narrows his eyes at me as he puts his hands on his hips. My eyes dip down to watch his abs move in and out as he breathes. He takes a few strides toward me so we're just feet apart.

"I wasn't expecting you," he says, and I swallow. He juts his head to the side. "Come on. Let me show you my favorite spot in this town."

I follow him across the field, wildflowers popping up in droves all around, bees humming by. The sky is a deep blue today with those big, cotton-ball type puffy clouds. And then we get to the edge of the field, and my jaw drops. The whole town is below us, the lake a dark blue-green, shimmering in the sunlight. Trees everywhere, houses popping out from every angle. Windmills miles and miles away in the mountains far out, cars on the highway. Boats making their own waves as they stream across the lake.

It's breathtaking, and I'm surprised at the emotional response I feel.

"Wow," I whisper, and before I realize it, he's standing right next to me.

"Yeah," he says back, a smile on his lips. "This is why none of us leave. This is why May loved it here."

I nod. I get it. He turns to me, and my stomach flips right on cue.

"I'm sorry I didn't come sooner, Kaylee," he tells me, his eyes on the ground. "I wish she had more time. I wish *you* had more time with her."

I swallow and instinctively reach out to grab his arm.

"No, no. I'm so glad you found me. Even if I didn't get to meet May, I'm so glad you brought me here, Derrick."

I turn back to the view.

"I can't believe I have a sister," I say, biting my lip. He nods.

"Yeah. Crazy. She's pretty great, though," he says with a shrug. "I really think you two would get along."

I let out a sarcastic laugh.

"She can't stand the sight of me."

"Kaylee," he says, rubbing the back of his neck, "the girl's been through a lot. Give her time. Besides, I doubt there's a person in the world who wouldn't like the sight of you."

He gives me a sly half-smile, and I feel tingles run down my whole body, fizzling out at the tips of my fingers. I inch closer to him, but I feel him pull back slightly.

There goes that bullshit again. But I refuse to let him off that easy. If he's going to dish out the one-liners, he better be prepared to take them.

"You're not so hard to look at, either," I tell him, an ache in my core sinking down between my legs. I want to trace the lines of his muscles, chase the drops of sweat down his broad back...

There's a long silence between us, then he shakes his head.

"Nah," he whispers, "I was *definitely* not expecting you." I tilt my head, perplexed, wondering why we can't just give in. Why he's not yanking my shorts down right here in this field, touching me everywhere, those perfectly round lips on mine...

Jesus. I guess it's safe to say I wasn't expecting him, either.

"You ready to head back?" he asks. I nod, taking one last look off the ledge, committing it all to memory like some sort of mental postcard. The way back is a relief, my body thanking me for the steady decline. As we hop over branches and roots again, I feel his hand on my lower back, guiding me gently.

We finally turn back onto May's street and come to a stop as we reach the driveway. We sit down on the porch, stretching our legs and catching our breath.

"So," he says, nudging me with his leg, "we goin' again tomorrow?"

I smile and nudge him back.

"Hell yeah."

13

I open the front door, kicking my shoes off on the porch, and make my way inside. I head for the kitchen and get a glass of water from the fridge, leaning up against the cool granite of the island as I gulp it down. I have no earthly idea how I'm going to do this again tomorrow, but for that view—both of the town and of him—I'd happily die all over again.

Just as I set the glass in the sink, I hear a thud coming from upstairs. I swallow, my heart jumping to my throat. There were no cars in the driveway when we got back. I shake my head, thinking it might be my mind playing tricks on me. Then I hear the slide of a drawer opening and closing again, and I'm back to panic mode.

I slowly walk into the living room toward the bottom of the stairs. I look around the room for something I can use as a weapon. A fire poker. Perfect. I reach to pull it out of the stand, but when I do, it hooks onto one of the other tools and sends the entire set crashing to the floor. I jump to try to gather them without making any more noise, but it's completely useless. When I turn back around, I see Haven standing at the top of the stairs. I jump back.

"Oh, shit!" I scream, clutching a hand to my chest. She doesn't say anything, just raises an eyebrow in my direction. "Sorry. I didn't know you were—"

"I knocked, but no one answered, so I let myself in. I'll be out of your hair in a minute. Just getting some clothes to take back to Alma's."

"Oh, you don't have to…" I start to say, but she turns and walks back into her bedroom. I consider leaving her be, but I decide to take advantage of being alone with her. I walk up the stairs and stand in her doorway. "You can stay as long as you want. This is *your* house," I tell her.

She scoffs as she folds some t-shirts and shoves them into a duffel bag.

"You met with Jeffrey, right?" she asks. I nod. "Then you know this is *your* house, too." There's something flippant about the way she says it, as if I don't deserve it.

Which I probably don't.

I turn to walk back down the steps but freeze.

"Look, I'm not here to tear apart your life, Haven. At least, not any more than I already have. I just…"

My voice trails off, and I see that she's stopped packing. Her back is to me, but she's completely still.

"Can we get lunch or something? Maybe? Just the two of us?" I ask. I swallow, feeling completely vulnerable. She thinks for a moment then turns so I can see the profile of her face. She nods her head slowly, and I let out a silent sigh of relief.

"You have to drive, though. I brought the boat."

"Sure," I tell her. "I'll just shower quick, and we can go."

. . .

WE GET IN THE CAR, and she gives me directions into town.

"Feel like anything in particular?" she asks. I shake my head.

"I eat just about anything," I say. She points out a small sandwich shop that sits on a pier on the water a few yards up. I veer off the highway and pull into the gravel lot.

"This place has the best subs in town," she says as we get out. I nod.

"Good to know."

We walk up to the ordering window, and as I stare at the menu, I hear her order two sandwiches.

"Hey, Mike," she says. "We'll take two turkey sandwiches on rye with chips on the side."

I look at her, and she shrugs. "You said you eat anything, right? You'll like it."

I smile and nod.

"Turkey it is."

Mike slides the food to us through the window, and I follow her to a table on the deck next to the railing, close to the water.

We eat in silence for a few minutes, watching the boats pass. She's right. This sandwich is good.

"So, you're in college, right?" I ask her, finally breaking the silence. No use in dancing around all the questions I have for her. If we're going to get to know each other at all, we have to start with the basics. She nods, picking a chip up and popping it into her mouth.

"Just finished my sophomore year. I go to Sinclair

University in Pennsylvania," she says. "It's about two hours away."

"What are you studying?" I ask her.

"Business," she says. "I want to come back here and pick up where May left off."

I swallow a big bite and take a sip of my water.

"That's really, uh, that's great," I say. I avoid the topic of me and my half of the inheritance. "I know we haven't talked much since I've been here, but I just wanted to say that I'm really sorry, Haven. My head is spinning from all of this, but I just...I can't imagine what that feels like, to lose the person who meant the most to you."

She stares straight ahead then sniffs and drops her crust back onto her plate. She nods slowly.

"She gave me the most wonderful life," she says, and that's when I realize her voice is cracking. She looks up at me, and I see the tears pooling in her eyes. I have the urge to reach out and take her hand, but I don't. She just finally agreed to be in the same vicinity as me for longer than a minute. I can't overstep right now.

"What was it like?"

Her eyes drop down to her hands on the table as she traces the knots in the wood with her index finger.

"It was magic," she says. "May was magic. We never argued. We were meant to live together, I think."

I smile weakly, but there's something about her words that stings my heart.

"She was strict, but only about things like my self-confidence. She wanted me to remember that I could do anything. And I did. I will."

She smiles, and I realize it's the first time I've seen her smile since I've been here. She's stunning, her bronze skin bright in the sun. Freckles are sprinkled across her nose, giving her a youthful look, but the pain behind her eyes shows she's seen some real hurt in her nineteen years.

"I remember this one time, I told her I wanted to paint my room. She offered to have painters come, but I told her I wanted to do it on my own. So, we went and bought all the supplies, and she walked me through it. When it came time to paint, she walked out of the room. I called after her, but she told me this was *my* project. I couldn't believe it. Left me to do it all myself when she could have helped me. It took me a month, but I got that damn room painted. Some of the carpet got painted, too, but at least it was done. And that's how she was with everything. She supported every dream I ever had and made sure I had the tools to reach it. But she also made sure I knew that *I* had to get it. No one else could do the work for me."

"It sounds like she had a good head on her shoulders."

Haven nods.

"The best. The way she changed this town, the way people looked at her, you just knew she was special. I'm so thankful she's the woman that raised me."

I swallow the lump in my throat. I know she means it as praise for May, but it also feels like it's a dig at my mother. At *our* mother.

I wait for her to ask me about her, to see what my life was like, but she doesn't.

"Man," I finally say after a long pause, "this is just all so surreal." Haven scoffs and pulls herself up onto the table, facing out over the lake. I follow suit and sit next to her, careful to leave a comfortable distance between us.

"You're telling me," she says.

"Did you...did you always know about me?" I ask. She nods.

"Always. May didn't keep secrets from me," she says. Another dig at my mom. But I can't say I blame her.

"I thought my parents didn't, either," I tell her. "But the longer I'm here, the more things seem to come to the surface."

Haven's eyes drop to the ground in front of us.

"I guess I was naive all those years," I say. "I mean, I knew they weren't always the happiest. But an affair? Another...another child?"

"And a black child, at that," she says matter-of-factly. "I guess it's been a tough few weeks for both of us."

We look at each other, and a sad smile crosses over my lips. Suddenly, a slow laugh escapes her.

"What?" I ask.

"Nothin'. Just funny. Like mother like daughter, I guess," she says with a shrug.

"What? What do you mean?"

She shoots me a knowing look.

"You might have only been here for a week or two," she says. "But we can all see what's goin' on with you and Derrick."

Her lips turn up mischievously, and I bite the corners of my mouth to try not to smile.

"What? I...no way. He's just... I don't even know what you're—"

"Nah, don't worry. Derrick doesn't date, really," she says, finally calming down. My shoulders sink in disappointment.

"Oh," I say.

"He's pretty guarded, actually. Seems to like you, though. Do me a favor. When you leave, let him down easy, okay?"

My eyes shoot to hers, and I don't know what cuts deeper—the idea that I'd be hurting Derrick, or the fact that she's so certain I'll be leaving.

14

We get back to the house, and Haven says a quick goodbye before disappearing down to the water. As I watch her leave, I'm surprised to feel a little bit of sadness come over me. I actually enjoyed my time with her today. And I want more.

Now, I'm lying on the couch in this giant living room in this giant house all by myself, wondering how the fuck I ended up here.

As I'm flicking through the channels on the giant flatscreen that hangs above the two-story stone fireplace, my phone buzzes on the end table next to me.

"Hello?" I ask.

"Kaylee, it's Jeff," his sing-song voice carries through the phone. "Listen, I got a call from May's finance guy a few minutes ago. It looks like he's almost done crunching all the numbers. I should have that full ledger for you tomorrow if you want to stop by the office and pick it up."

"Oh, that would be great," I tell him. "Looking forward to seeing what May was doing."

"She was changing the world," he says. "Well, Meade Lake's world, anyway. See you tomorrow, sweetie."

I decide to "unpack" the few things I have in my drawers and explore the house a little more. There's a study on the main level with a huge oak desk and floor-to-ceiling, built-in bookshelves. It looks like the books are sorted by genre. I poke around the non-fiction but settle on a romance novel. As I pluck it from the shelves, it sends the two books on either side of it crashing to the ground. I bend down to pick them up and see a box on the lower level. It has my mother's name written across it in big black letters, and I freeze. I pull the box from its spot and carry it out to the living room. I set it on the giant coffee table and pull the lid off. The box is full of books and envelopes and stacks of photos.

I pull out one of the books and read the front. MILLSTOWN HIGH SCHOOL is carved into the leather. I flip through the pages until I find my mother. Her hair is teased in that 80s fashion, her sleeves a bit poofier than I would wear now. Her face is rounder, more full of life. But it's the smile that gets me—so big and wide and real. I have never seen this smile on my mother's face. Ones I've seen have been forced and plastered on at a company event or in public somewhere. Even behind the scenes, when it was just she and I, the relaxed version of the smile she had seemed to have something weighing on it. Now I know what that was.

When I see her name, it stops me in my tracks: *Karnie Dean.* Dean. Before she became Karnie Jennings.

Before she became Duke Jennings' wife, and the rest of her identity was sealed up in a trophy-wife package sealed with a ribbon that was too tight to ever unravel. Even when an affair and a surprise baby tried to cut through it.

I flick through the book, looking for her in the pictures of the clubs and sports, laughing, hugging friends. When I flip to the back, I see loads of scribbled notes that her friends signed. And then I see one that takes up half a page.

DEAR KARNIE,

I know we don't know where the rest of our lives will take us. I know that when you go off to college next year, I'll still be here in Millstown. But I know that, someday, our lives are going to cross again. You're the love of my life, Karnie Dean.

Your Billy

I FLIP through the pages of the yearbook, searching for a *William*, or a *Bill*, or a *Billy*. And then I land on him. Billy Walter, a handsome black man toward the end of Mom's class. He has this smile that lights up his whole face. His hair was styled in a bit of a fade then, and I freeze when I see his eyes. Big and round and brown. Sort of like Haven's.

I look into the box and see a huge envelope stuffed with pieces of paper. When I pull them out, I realize they're letters to my mom. There are a few that are in similar fashion as the yearbook note. Young, innocent.

Then there are a few more that are dated into her

college years and even after I know she was already with my dad.

Dear Karnie,

I know things are harder. We can't see each other much. I know you're with him. But you should know that I don't sleep without you. I wake up every day thinking about what I can do to make the world better for you. What I can do to make my world something you might be a part of again one day.

I know he has it all, Karnie. But one day, I'll be able to give you everything you need.

Your Billy

I FEEL this weird twist in my stomach as I read. It feels a little too personal reading these, like I'm violating their privacy. But I can't stop.

The next letter is dated the year I turned four. The year before Haven was born.

Dear Karnie,

I know it's dangerous to send this to the house. I wasn't sure how else to get in touch with you. Karnie, I'm ready for you. I've made my money. I got a house now, Karnie. When we were together last month, I told you I was close. I know you got that big old house now, and he can pay for whatever it is that you need. But I know you know that what we have isn't something you can buy. I'll love your little girl, Karnie, because she's got you in her. If you want to work, I'm happy to stay home with her. If you want to stay home, I'll work. You can be the best version of you with me.

I know you know that night we were together will be the best night of your life, just like it will be for me. And if it's the last night I ever spend with you, if that was the last time I'll ever see you, I'll hold onto it forever. This will be my last letter to you, Karnie. I can't put myself through it anymore, and I won't risk causing any damage to your marriage if it's what you truly want. My number is on the inside of the envelope. If you're ever ready, call me.

Your Billy

TEARS POOL in my eyes as I reread them. His handwriting is hard and thick, like he pressed into the paper with agony as he wrote. I dig through the box, trying to find the original envelope that the letter was in, but there's nothing, and no return address on the other envelope.

I feel a lump in my throat as I sink back to the floor, crouched down, staring at the bleeding ink on the pages in front of me, thinking of the bleeding heart that wrote them. And I think of my parents, and their marriage, their relationship. The surface-level bullshit I've witnessed my whole life with no real depth. I think of the lies they told to each other, the lies they told to me. And how the daughter of this woman, who once had a man love her so deeply, who opened his heart to loving *me* for her, sits on the floor of a giant lake house all alone, wondering how the fuck this all came to be.

I reach my hand up to cover my mouth, the tears stinging my eyes as they drop from the corners. I don't even hear the front door open. I don't even hear the creak of the hardwoods as he rushes across them.

"Hey, hey," Derrick says, kneeling down in front of me. "What is it? What happened?"

I startle, my eyes settling on his as I calm myself down. He leans forward and cups my cheek, swiping a tear away with his thumb. I swallow nervously as he glances around at the box and the letters that are strewn around me. Before I know it, he takes hold of my hand and pulls me into his chest, holding me tight to him while I cry—something I *desperately* need to do. We sit like that for a few moments, him holding the back of my head, me lying against the hard peaks of his chest.

Finally, I clear my throat, his hand still on my cheek like he's holding me steady.

"I found these when I was in the study," I tell him. "Things of my mom's. And in them, I found these letters. I think they might be from...from Haven's father."

Derrick's eyes grow wide as he falls back against the floor, looking around.

"What do they say?"

I scoff.

"A lot of things I've never come *close* to hearing my father say to her. 'You're the love of my life. I don't sleep without you,'" I say, shrugging, holding the letters up. "I've never heard my parents tell each other they love each other, let alone anything like *this*. My parents don't have *this.*" I throw the letters and the book back into the box and push it away from me. "I don't think they ever did. And I always knew that, I think. But they seemed to have it all together, you know? They seemed to have everything they needed in each other. Never wanting for anything. But then I see *these*, and I realize, all along, she actually had *nothing*. She gave this up; she gave up someone wanting her like that. For *what?* She gave her *child* up. Because she wasn't the right shade? Because he wasn't a CEO?"

My hands shake, and I realize how loud I am, as if screaming these questions into the air could somehow make my mother hear them in Lenburn.

"It's hard when people disappoint us," he says, scooting over toward me and leaning back against the couch. "Especially when it's the people we know best."

I look at him and cock my head, wondering what experience he has with this.

"You know, I've been thinking a lot about my dad's company. About this stupid manager role I'm supposed to be taking. You know there are fifteen executives at the company, and they're all white? There's this man there, Franklin. He's been there since my dad opened the doors back in the nineties. So loyal. So intelligent in the tech world. He should be up there on that team."

"Have you ever mentioned Franklin to your dad?" he asks me. I nod.

"Yeah. But he always has a reason, ya know? Something that makes another candidate more qualified. And when I look at it now, even when there are other people hired who aren't white, they never seem to make it past the managerial level. It's almost like it's…"

"Systemic," he says, finishing my sentence better than I could. I nod slowly.

"Yeah," I choke out. "This whole time, my whole life, I knew my parents weren't perfect. But I thought they were pretty damn close. They always wanted what was best for me. They always bought me the best clothes, the most expensive computer, the best cars. Whatever I could have ever wanted. But through all of that, I was blind to everything else. Man, I've been such a naive idiot."

He nudges his shoulder against mine, rubbing his hands on his jeans.

"That's the trouble when the people you love hurt you," he says. "You don't recognize it as hurt right away, because you can't even fathom them being capable of doing it."

I nod slowly.

"I'm supposed to take that job," I say just above a whisper. "I'm supposed to get one of those corner offices and be in charge of people who have more qualifications than I do. I'm supposed to decide if they get *raises*. Their whole damn livelihood. I'm supposed to be...*him.*"

Derrick lifts his hand and covers mine, pulling it over to him.

"Kaylee," he says, looking down into my eyes. "The fact that you're sitting here right now, telling me this, realizing all of this about the people who raised you, tells me that you are not like your father. Or your mother. You're like May."

My eyebrows shoot up. His eyes dip down from mine to my lips, and his tongue juts out to wet his own. I feel this pull, and I press myself up closer to him, moving as near to him as possible without being on top of him. I reach my hand up to his face, and he swallows nervously. I feel his breath quicken as I pull myself closer to him.

But as my hand lands on his cheek, he takes it and brings it gently to his lips. My eyes fall, and so does my stomach.

"Kaylee, I..." he says, his voice drifting off. He kisses the back of my hand, and a chill shoots down my back. He shakes his head, and my hand drops from his lips. I push myself back, feeling vulnerable, exposed, and a little bit pissed off.

"What is it, Derrick?" I ask him. I've had enough bullshit from my parents to last me a lifetime. I don't really need any more. "You check on me, you touch me, but every time things feel like they might go a *little* bit further…"

He pushes himself up to his feet as he stalks toward the deck doors. He puts a hand on the wood as he stares out over the black water. I follow him, wrapping my arms around my body.

"Kaylee, I've wanted to touch you since the moment you walked into my hotel room in Georgia."

I clear my throat.

"Then…why don't you? I'm a big girl, Derrick. Believe it or not, I won't fall apart if you touch me. And if we never touch again after that? I'll be just fine. I've had plenty of guys in my lifetime do just that."

His eyes meet mine, and the serious look in them makes me step back.

"Any man that gets to touch you, and chooses to only touch you once, is a damn fool."

I swallow, and he takes a step closer to me.

"And I promise you that if I ever did touch you, it wouldn't be one and done. If I touched you, you'd feel everything you deserve to feel, over and over again. I wouldn't stop until I knew every inch of you was touched the way it should be."

I'm one step away from panting now, and I can't remember the last time I've been this sexually frustrated. I want him in an animalistic way, like throw-me-over-his-shoulder-and-march-me-to-the-bedroom   kind   of way. But in a jolting stop to my libido, he reaches out for my hand again, interlocking our fingers.

"But I can't do that to you, Kaylee." His eyes drop to the floor. "It's not fair to you; it's not fair to May. I can't be in your head. I'm sorry."

He kisses my hand one more time, and as he walks out the front door, I stare down at my hand as if a brand of his lips is going to appear.

15

While I've done a fairly good job of it over the last few months, while dude after dude left me disappointed in the bedroom, I'm convinced that sex with myself is never going to be as amazing as I picture it would be with Derrick.

Those bulging arms wrapped around me, my legs up over his shoulders.

Ugh. I drown myself in freezing cold water before turning the faucet off and hopping out to dry off.

I shove a granola bar into my mouth as I head out the door and hop in May's Explorer. My silver BMW still sits in the driveway, but I haven't so much as unlocked the door since I got May's keys.

My phone tells me to turn right onto Lakeshore Highway and drive for two miles. Boats cross the water parallel to me on the road, and big puffy clouds move to make a little bit of shade. I put all the windows down as I drive, inhaling the fresh air and letting it fill my lungs with a fullness I haven't had in a long time.

I drive farther, and on my right, I see the strip where

Big Moon Sports sits, Derrick's truck parked in front. I wonder what he'd do if I pulled over and kicked the door open, demanding he explain himself or finish the job he started.

But I get myself together and continue on my mission.

Finally, the phone tells me to turn left a little past Lou's and then make an immediate right into a small lot that sits in front of a building that looks like a house. Every building in this town seems to have those giant floor-to-ceiling windows, but I guess when nature provides such a beautiful backdrop, a wall is almost an insult.

Inside Jeffrey's office, a young woman sits at a desk in the lobby, clicking away on a keyboard. She greets me with a million-dollar smile.

"Hi, can I help you?" she asks.

"Uh, yes. I'm here to see Jeffrey Tate. My name's—"

"Miss Jennings?" she cuts me off. "I'm Tara, Mr. Tate's assistant. You can follow me back."

She's tall and slim with long legs and calf muscles that flex with every step of her black pumps. Her high-waisted skirt accentuates how tiny she is. She wears glasses with thick brown frames, and her chestnut hair is pulled up into a perfect ponytail, not a bump or loose hair in sight.

I follow her down a hallway to the last door on the right side where she taps once and pushes it open.

"She's here," she says.

"There she is!" Jeffrey says, that sing-song voice making me feel all warm inside. "Thank you, Tara. Can you cancel the rest of my appointments today and reschedule for tomorrow? Paul and I are taking the rest of the afternoon off. It's too nice of a day not to be on the water."

I look out the window at the water, the dull buzzing of a boat's motor still loud enough to be heard. Tara leaves us, and he holds out his hand to the leather couch in the back of his office. He takes a seat in the leather chair that's adjacent to me, crossing his legs as he lays out a large file on the table in front of us.

"So, all the dirty secrets are right here in this book," he says, opening the file with a smirk. I smile.

"Dirty, huh?"

He shakes his head.

"Naw, I'm just kidding. May did everything by the book. So, there's a master list here of all the money that May lent out, was in the process of recollecting, and that she planned to lend."

I look up at him.

"Planned to?" He nods. "So, what happens to those businesses now?"

"You do. *You* happen to them," he says. I look at him and lift an eyebrow. "Sorry to dump all this on you, sweetie. But until Haven graduates from college two years from now, you are the only heiress who has freedom with her inheritance at this moment."

I nod and swallow.

"So, here's the master list," he says, flipping to one of the first pages, "that'll show you the names of every company she has had past, present, or future business with. Then, each company or business has its own separate file that will give you the details of the repayment and where they stand. May's financial advisor will go through the nitty-gritty of this with you, if and when you're ready for the details."

I look down the list, names jumping out at me that I recognize. Lou's—but I knew that story there. I can see that May lent him the loan to purchase the building, and it looks like, a few years back, she gave him another small loan to add on a second deck.

I also notice that May put some money into the little bed and breakfast I stayed in when I first got here, around the time when the resort opened from what Derrick told me.

There are some other shops and restaurants, a cafe, and a bakery in town. A few she lent a few thousand dollars to, either for a repair or for a small upgrade. To others, she lent large sums for purchasing or renting bigger spaces or to help them start up.

Looking through the basics, it looks like she never collected interest, and there was no set timeframe on when the repayment needed to be complete.

I scan the rest of the list, and my eyes freeze when I see Big Moon Sports. I flip to the individual file for the store, and my heart freezes in my chest for a moment.

The agreed upon sum will be lent to owners Ryder Casey and Derrick Thomas for improvements and expansion of Big Moon Sports.

I swallow and reread his name a few times.

He doesn't just work at the store. He *owns* it. And May was supposed to be giving him more money.

I close the book up and stuff it into my bag.

"Thanks, Jeffrey. For everything. I'll look through this and see where she was, and I'll get back in touch with you for the finance guy's name," I tell him. He stands as I do. I stick out a hand, but he takes it and pulls me in for a hug instead.

"Sweetheart, I know this is a lot. I know that's all we

keep saying to you," he says. "So, if you have any questions, or concerns, or just need to go get a damn drink, call me."

I smile and nod and walk out of his office, nodding to Tara as I make my way back to the Explorer.

As I speed back down Lakeshore Highway, I pull off into the strip where Big Moon Sports is perched on the side of the water.

There's a line out the door for people waiting to rent boats and jet skis and people crossing the street to the dock, heading out for theirs. I turn into the store and see Ryder and Mila behind the counter.

"Hey, lady!" Mila calls, scrambling to grab form after form and handing customer after customer pens.

"Hi," I say, taking in the commotion around me. "Is Derrick in today?"

She looks up at me, a smirk on her face.

"Down by the docks," Ryder says, sliding around the front of the counter. He uses his cane to walk toward me. "Everything okay?"

"Yeah, um, fine."

I turn to walk back out the door but turn back.

"You guys didn't tell me you owned this place."

Ryder's eyebrows jump.

"I take it you saw the ledger," he says.

"Yeah." He lets out a long sigh.

"Derrick didn't want to complicate things. You should...you should talk to him."

I nod slowly.

"I plan to. Thanks, Ryder," I say, reaching for the door.

"Kaylee?" he asks. I turn back to him. "Go easy on the guy, okay?"

I nod again and make my way out across the street.

On the dock, Derrick is walking in and out of a shed-like structure that sits on top of it, pulling life vests out of it and handing them to the customers. He's untying boats, shoving them off, giving instructions, and keeping everything moving.

I assume he works out here a lot. I'm not sure how Ryder could manage this part of the business safely.

After he pushes the last group out and waves them off, he catches a glimpse of me and stands straight up. I swallow, unsure how this exchange is going to go. After all, the last time we spoke, he basically told me that if we ever slept together, he'd make love to every inch of my body. Not real sure how to recover from that.

"Hey," he says, shielding his eyes from the sun. He's wearing a cut-off t-shirt that's wet from water, and maybe sweat, and is sticking to the curves of his muscles. His hair is slightly longer on the top of his head than everywhere else, and it looks more curly right now than usual.

"Hi," I say, walking toward him.

"Careful now," he says with a slick smile, "I've seen you fall off one or two of these before." I stop in my tracks and put my hand on my hip, shooting him a look.

"Busy day out here, huh?" I ask, looking out over the busy water when I reach the end.

"Yeah," he says. "Business is great right now." He bends down to secure the rope on one of the jet skis.

"So, is that why you were trying to expand?" He stands slowly and turns around to me, his eyes narrowed and penetrating. "Why didn't you tell me you owned this place? And that May was supposed to be giving you guys a loan?"

He walks by me and into the shed, stacking the extra life vests and hanging some on hooks. I follow behind him and lean against the doorway.

"Derrick, I could take all this money and walk away from here. And you knew that the whole time, but you still came to get me. Why? If you had just let the time run out, the money would roll up and go back to the businesses."

He hangs the last stack of vests up and turns back to me, leaning against the wall behind him.

"It's not my money," he says matter-of-factly, "and it's not my decision what happens to it. May needed you, so I had to try."

I lean my head to the side.

"But even when she died, you asked me to come back." He nods.

"Because by then, I'd already walked in and rattled your whole world. Let you in on a few crazy secrets. How could I leave you like that?"

He takes a few steps in my direction and looks down at me, his eyes tracing my lips before moving back up to mine.

"I looked at you, and I saw this girl who'd been lied to her whole life. I wanted to...I *still* want to take care of that. And you."

His eyes are still narrowed on mine, and I cower a bit under his gaze.

"You're....you're incred—"

"Don't go saying things you don't know are true," he says, waving his arm. "I just tried to do what May would do. And once you walked into my hotel room, I kinda didn't like the idea of you going back."

He flashes me this devious half-smile that makes that fire build in my stomach again. I

tuck a piece of hair behind my ear.

"Well, I like being here," I say honestly, and his eyes widen a little bit. "I think I'm going to stick around for a little bit. I want to meet some of the business owners May was working with, discuss some things. See what her plans were."

A wider smile slithers over his lips.

"Oh yeah?" he says. I nod.

"Yeah. Starting with this store called Big Moon Sports. Ever heard of it?" I ask.

"Naw," he says, shaking his head as he steps closer to me so we're just inches apart. I

swallow as I let him invade my space. "But I hear the owner is kind of a pain." He puts his hand up to the side of my head, resting it on the door jamb. He's so close I can smell him, this sweet, musty smell of being out on the fresh water and in the sun all day.

"Man, what a shame. I was gonna see if he wanted to finish what he started." His lips part slightly as his eyes widen.

I surprise myself with my prowess, but I play it off. After giving him my best attempt at a seductive smile, I turn and walk out of the shed, back toward the edge of the dock.

"Hey," he calls after me. I turn back slowly. "If he starts back up again, he may never

want to stop." The look on his face is playful, but I can see the look in his eyes, like he's a hunter. I swallow and nod.

"Bring it."

He chuckles to himself, hanging his head.

"You got plans tomorrow?" he asks. I laugh.

"What plans would I have?"

"Good point. You want to go out on the water? I can take you around to some of the

other spots May was working with. We can see if some of the crew wants to come, make

a day of it.

"That sounds great."

"Good."

I turn on my heel and head back up to my car, my insides already churning in

anticipation.

16

The next morning, I shower and blow dry my hair, trying to tame my waves a bit without making it look like I'm trying too hard. Most girls can master that natural, beachy wave, no-makeup look. For me, I end up looking like a toddler who woke too early from a nap.

I slip into a tight-fitting tank and some shorter-than-normal shorts and head downstairs to wait for Derrick. No sooner than I step foot into the living room is there a knock at the door. Before I get to the foyer, he's let himself in.

"Hey, hey," he says, his familiar greeting making me jumpy. He hands me an iced coffee as he walks toward me.

"Wasn't sure what you liked, so I got it black and brought some cream and sugar," he says, handing me a little baggie. I smile and nod.

"Thanks. It's perfect like this," I say, holding the cup up before I take a sip. "You want to come in for a bit?" He shakes his head.

"Nope. The gang's all waitin' for us." My eyebrows perk up.

"The gang?" He smiles and nods his head toward the back door.

"Come on," he says. I grab my purse and lock the front door behind us, heading for his truck. But he pauses and grabs my arm, leading me around toward the back of the house.

"They're picking us up here," he says, pulling me down toward the water. His fingers linger on my skin, leaving a zinging trail in their wake.

"Who's 'they'?" I ask just as we get to the dock. I see a pontoon boat tied up at the end of it, a bunch of smiling faces looking back at us. Teddy's in the driver's seat, and to his left sits Haven. At the front of the boat, Ryder sits with Annabelle on his lap, and Mila sits next to him, sipping out of a red cup.

"Yo, let's do this!" Teddy calls to us.

"We're picking up Jules and Luna," Mila calls back to us. I look at Derrick.

"*This* is the gang," he says, stepping aside as we reach the boat and holding his hand out to me. He lifts me on, and I take a seat at the back of the boat, waving to everyone. He unties the boat from the dock and settles in the seat next to me.

"No bathing suit?" Mila asks. I look around at all of them with swim trunks and bikini ties sticking out from their clothes. I shrug.

"I didn't exactly come prepared," I say.

"Yeah, that's okay. You don't need a suit to get wet," Derrick says, and my lips part at his double-entendre. "Let's go!"

Teddy turns the key in the ignition, and the boat

jumps to life. Mila and Derrick hop up to pull up the bumpers as we back out, and then we're off, Gran May's house shrinking in the background behind us.

It's a gorgeous day; it's hot but not Georgia hot. There's a cool crispness to this air, even on the hottest of days, that makes it bearable. And being on the water makes it even better. I look in Haven's direction, but she's staring off the side of the boat, her knees pulled up to her chest on the seat.

"Hay," Derrick calls to her. She turns around slowly to look at him. "Smile."

They exchange looks, and she does. I'm convinced it's impossible to see that grin and not send one back in return. He leans forward and pulls her into a hug, leaving loud kisses on her cheeks. She makes a fake vomiting sound and pushes him off playfully before he sinks back into the seat next to me. I'm envious of their relationship and the way Haven leans on him. Like he's a brother.

A couple zips by us on a jet ski, and a teenaged kid skates by on water skis, making it look like he could do it in his sleep. Derrick and the crew wave to a few people as we ride along. "Daddy, I wanna sit near the driver's seat!" Annabelle calls from the front of the boat.

"Oh, you do, huh?" Ryder says with a smirk as he ruffles her hair.

"Here, baby girl," Haven says, standing up from her seat, "you can have my spot." She holds her hand out to Annabelle who walks down toward her and takes it. Haven lifts her into the seat before turning around to look for somewhere to go.

I scoot to my side and point to the spot next to me.

"Here," I offer, "there's plenty of room." She looks

at me skeptically, then to Derrick, then reluctantly takes it, clearing her throat as she does.

"So," she says, to my surprise, "how are you liking the house?"

"It's amazing," I tell her. "It must have been so cool growing up there."

A smile spreads across Haven's lips as she looks out to the mountains.

"It was a damn dream," she mutters. A breeze blows by, and she closes her eyes, letting it blow over her.

"Look, I don't want to make you feel like you can't be there or put you out. If you're not comfortable with us both staying there, I'm happy to go back to the inn. I'm still paying for my room, so I still have it."

She looks at me and flashes me another quick smile.

"Nah, it's not just you," she says. "I'm not ready to be there without her yet."

I nod slowly, letting her words sink in.

It's funny. She doesn't know the house—or life, for that matter—without May. I don't know it *with* her.

"Why are you still paying for the room?" Derrick asks, leaning back to extend his arm across the back of the seat so that his fingers dangle just above my shoulder.

"I, uh, I didn't want Mrs. Miller to lose the business so soon," I say. He narrows his eyes on me as that devious smile tugs at the corner of his mouth.

"Should we pull off for a quick dip?" Teddy asks, pointing the boat toward a cove. "It's hot out here."

We pull a little farther down, and he cuts the engine. The boat floats around slowly, and Teddy and Ryder are stripping off their shirts and jumping off the boat within seconds. Mila helps Annabelle zip up her life vest, and she gets a running start off the boat into the deep, dark water.

Haven slips her t-shirt off before taking an Olympic-level dive into the water. Derrick stands next to me. He reaches his hands down slowly to the hem of his shirt before pulling it off his head. I try not to stare, but it's really fucking hard.

"You comin'?" he asks. I swallow and shake my head, pointing to my body.

"No suit, remember?"

He leans down close to me so that his lips are mere inches from my ear.

"I thought I told you I could get you wet with no problem."

I swallow, and before I realize what he's doing, he wraps his arms around my waist and scoops me up. He shakes my feet so that my sandals fall from them into the boat, then he stands on the back.

"Here we come!" he calls out, and the rest of the group cheers from the water. *Traitors.* I scream as he jumps, holding my breath as we get sucked under. The sensation of the chilly lake water combined with the heat of his body sends my hormones raging. He wraps his arm around my waist again and pushes up to the surface. I laugh and push my hair back out of my face.

"You looked like you were getting kinda hot," he says with a wink. I splash him.

"Jerk," I laugh as I swim to the ladder that hangs off the back of the boat.

We swim for a little while, jumping and diving, treading water and lounging on the back

of the boat. Derrick and I catch each other's eyes more than once, and each time, it makes my heart jump. He made it clear that he won't be crossing any physical line any time soon, but it sure does feel like that line is getting more blurry by the day. Just as he's narrowed in on me, swimming in my direction, Annabelle pipes up.

"Mama, I have to use the bathroom," she says as she kicks toward the boat.

"Number one or number two?" Mila asks. Annabelle looks around to all of us before leaning a little closer to her.

"Number two," she says in her best attempt at a whisper.

"No problem," Teddy says with a chuckle. "Let's go. I'll whip it back around, and we can go toward town. We could use some provisions, anyway."

One by one, we all climb back in. Derrick tosses me a towel, and I dry off a bit before taking my seat next to him again. Teddy points the boat toward shore where a few small businesses sit, and I recognize the cafe that Derrick pointed out next to what looks to be a convenience store.

"What can I get everyone?" Mila asks as Teddy pulls the boat into one of the slots.

"I can run into the store while you take her," Haven says, pulling her t-shirt back on over her bathing suit. I look from her to Mila.

"I can come, too," I say. Haven looks at me for a moment then nods. We get the rest of the crew's snack orders, and then I follow her and Mila off the boat, down the dock, and up the set of wooden stairs that lead up the hillside to where the convenience store sits.

We part ways with Mila and Annabelle, and they head off to use the bathroom at the cafe while we go to grab the food. I follow Haven inside as she scrolls through the list of orders she took on her phone.

"Jeesh, Derrick asked for the whole damn store," she says with a chuckle. "I don't know how someone can eat as much as he does and also *look* the way he does."

I smile, picturing his body when he slipped that shirt off just a little while ago.

"You can stop drooling now," she says, and I snap back to reality and shake my head.

"Uh, what—what do you mean?"

She scoffs.

"Girl, please. He might be like my brother, but it doesn't mean I don't see how girls look at him. It's not a secret he looks like some damn model." She turns down the first aisle to grab some chips, and I follow behind.

"Are there, uh, are there a lot of, um…" My cheeks begin to burn as my eyes drop down to my feet. She turns to face me.

"You tryin' to get the deets on him?" she asks, perching a hand on her hip and looking at me. I swallow. But then her face breaks into a sly smile. "The deets are…there are none. Derrick is very guarded. His parents had a rocky relationship. It's sort of a long story and not mine to tell. But the short of it is, no, there's no one serious in Derrick's life. He's sort of Meade Lake's most eligible bachelor, but as long as I've known him, it's been nothing but short flings."

I nod slowly, feeling some sense of relief. "Don't worry. His eyes are on someone, alright. But that someone is you."

She turns at the end of the aisle and keeps walking. I grab the back half of the list, a water bottle for myself, and some sunflower seeds before walking back toward the front of the store. Haven emerges from the back, arms full of snacks and drinks, and lays them on the counter. As she reaches for her wallet, I put my hand on hers and slip the cashier my credit card.

"Let me. You all have been so amazing these last few weeks," I say before she can protest. "It's the least I can do for all the catching up you've had to do."

I can see she's questioning it, but after a moment, she puts the last of the items down and backs away from the counter so I can finish checking out. We turn to walk out when she freezes.

"Shoot. I forgot to get a popsicle for Annabelle. I'll meet you outside," she tells me before turning back inside. I'm standing in the parking lot for what seems to be too long. I look down the hill, and I can see that Mila and Annabelle are already back in the boat. I turn back to the store, and I see Haven, her hands up, standing directly in front of the counter. I burst back in through the door.

"What's going on?" I ask. Her eyes grow wide, and she shakes her head slowly, as if she wants me not to say anything.

"There's nothing to see, ma'am," says a new cashier who is standing behind the counter. He's got one hand up, his index finger pointed in Haven's direction. She's frozen, her hands up, as if it's a gun. His other is holding the phone to his ear, and I can hear him calling 911.

"Hello, yes, I believe I have an attempted robbery at Phil's Convenience off Lakeshore Highway. Yes, we're located up by the Sellbrooke Cafe. Suspect is a young woman, appears to be, uh, African American. Yes. Thank you."

He hangs the phone up, and I suddenly feel sick to

my stomach. But I also feel something else. Something that's making the blood run hot like lava through my veins. Something that's making my extremities numb.

"What the hell is going *on?*" I ask again. "She didn't take anything."

"I saw her," the man says.

"I didn't take anything, sir," Haven says, holding her hands up. "I was trying to get a popsicle, but it looks like you're out. That's all—"

"I saw you stuff something in your pocket before you walked toward that door," he says, his plump cheeks reddening with anger. He's got one hand on the counter and one down behind it, out of sight. He's overweight with a t-shirt that wraps tight around his belly before tucking into his jeans. He has a bushy, strawberry-blonde beard that looks like it's seen better days and a toothpick hanging out of his mouth.

"She wouldn't steal anything," I say again, taking a step closer.

"Ma'am, just go about your business, please," he says, never taking his eyes off Haven. Like he's afraid she's going to explode. "No one's comin' up in here and taking anything for free. I work too damn hard in this store." He narrows his eyes at her, and I see her swallow. Since the day I stepped foot in Meade Lake, Haven has been cold, then warmer, then funny, and even a little bit welcoming. But the one thing that's been consistent the whole time I've been here is that she's been fierce as hell. She loves the people around her fiercely; she loves the town fiercely. And I can tell she loved May fiercely. But right now, when I look at my sister, I see something I haven't seen her exhibit yet: fear.

My sister is scared.

"Haven…" I start to say. But she shakes her head at me.

"He has a shotgun back there," she says, her voice low and steady. She never takes her eyes from him. "I heard him cock it."

Everything around me goes silent, and all I can hear are my own shallow breaths. I don't know what to do. I move in slow motion, put my bags down on the counter, and take a few more steps closer to her so that I'm positioning myself between her and the checkout counter. She shakes her head subtly again, like she wants me to just disappear.

"This is my sister," I say, my voice getting louder. And for the first time, the man's eyes leave Haven as they dart to me. "And she didn't take anything."

Out of the corner of my eye, I can see the flashing lights of a police cruiser pull up out front of the doors. I swallow. A moment later, an officer walks in the door, pulling his pants up by his belt.

"Afternoon, Wayne," he says, nodding to the cashier. *Great. Everyone knows everyone in this town.* "What seems to be the problem here?"

"This one walked to the back of my store then went to walk out without buyin' anything. Saw her sticking something in her pocket as she headed for the door," he says, a smug look appearing on his face.

My palms are sweaty, and I'm fuming.

"Officer, this is my sister. She didn't take anything, she—"

The cop nods and holds his hand up.

"If you don't mind, ma'am, can you empty your pockets?" he asks, cutting me off. The ding of the bell above the door goes off, and I can see Ryder and Derrick walking in, Derrick leading Ryder in.

"What's going on?" Ryder asks, his voice booming. I feel a sense of relief when I see them. But to my surprise, Derrick slinks behind Ryder a bit.

"Nothin' to see here," Wayne says. "Please continue on with your shopping."

"I'm with them," Ryder says, nodding in our direction. "So I'll ask again: what's the problem here?" I know all he can see are shapes and colors, but there's no mistaking the anger in his eyes right now. And the look on Derrick's is one I have never seen in the few weeks I've known him. A heavy, pained anger, but also a hopelessness. Like he feels completely powerless. Our eyes lock for a moment, and then he drops his to the floor. I can see him drawing in long, slow breaths like he's trying to control himself.

"Caught this one," he says, jutting a thumb toward Haven, "trying to walk out without paying." Ryder takes a few more steps in our direction so that he's just feet away from Wayne.

"Ryder," Haven says in that same slow, steady voice, "he has a shotgun."

I swear, flames ignite in Ryder's eyes. He takes another few steps closer to Wayne, like he's made of fucking steel. Like a shotgun wouldn't blow him in half at this distance.

"Sir, I'm going to have to ask you to raise both hands above the counter, please," the officer interjects. Slowly, Wayne drags his other hand up and rests it on the counter—empty.

"Do you know who 'this *one*' is?" Ryder asks him. Wayne's beady eyes dart from Haven back to Ryder, and

he shakes his head. "This here is Haven. Haven *Dean*."
Wayne's eyes widen.

"Shit," he mutters under his breath as his eyes jump
from person to person in the store. Ryder plants his
hands on the counter in front of him.

"Granddaughter of May Dean that you have your
fucking hand on a gun for. And she didn't take anything
from your stupid fucking store."

Haven reaches into the pockets of her jean shorts
and pulls them out, showing the police officer that
they're completely empty.

"I don't steal," she says, her eyes drilling into Wayne.
He clears his throat and shifts awkwardly on his feet.

"Well, seems like all is okay here. Have a good day,
folks," the officer says. He's waiting for us to exit the
store before he leaves. Ryder sticks his hand out to
Haven, who takes it shakily. He pulls her in, and they
walk out the front door. Derrick follows behind, but not
before staring at Wayne again. I can see there is so much
he wants to say, but he knows, for some reason, he can't.

I walk toward the door and turn back to Wayne one
more time. He's standing still, like he's been stunned by
some sort of taser.

"That was wrong of you, and I think you know
that," I tell him. "She has to live with what you just put
her through. But so do you."

In the parking lot, Haven's leaning on Derrick's
shoulder as Ryder watches them from a few yards away.
I walk up next to him.

"That was…" I start, struggling to find the words.

"Really fucking unfair," he finishes my sentence for
me. "But that's their life. Even here."

17

The boat ride back is silent and awkward. We're on the open water, the wind whipping through us, but the air is still thick with tension. I replay the last minutes in my mind, over and over. I was angry. *So* angry. And stunned. *Completely* stunned.

But Haven and Derrick looked scared. Like something had silenced them.

No one speaks for a long time until, finally, Derrick leans across the seat and puts his hand on Haven's knee. She has her head turned to the side, looking out over the side of the boat.

"You good?" he asks her. She nods her head but doesn't turn to look at him. "They can't keep us down, Hay." She nods again, putting her hand on top of his and patting it. Finally, I start to recognize the scenery a little more, the one tree that stands taller than all the rest on the crest of the mountain ahead of us, a few of the massive houses I remember riding by. Teddy pulls the boat into the dock slip at May's, and I stand to collect my things. I thank them all for the day, but I'm met by forced smiles and quiet goodbyes. Mila pushes up from her seat and walks toward the back of the boat. She grabs Haven's hands and kneels down in front of her.

"We got you," she whispers before wrapping Haven in a hug. She takes the seat next to her and puts her arm around her shoulders, and I feel that same jealousy again that I felt when I watched her and Derrick. Like she's everyone else's sister, but mine.

Our eyes meet, and I nod in Haven's direction.

"I'm really sorry that happened to you today," I tell her, keeping my eyes trained on hers. I want her to know how much I mean it. How I'll be replaying that scene in my head over and over. She nods back at me.

"That's life, Kaylee," she says with a shrug as she leans back a bit in her seat. "You got our mom, but you also got something else out of that deal." I raise my eyebrows at her, and she nods in my direction again. "That skin. That skin will get you a lot of free passes in this world."

I look down at my arms as if I'm not aware what color my own flesh is. But that's just the thing; I've never thought about it. Not once. I look down at the light-brown freckles that speckle my pale skin, turning my arms over like I've just become aware of some sort of secret weapon I possess.

Our eyes meet one last time before I step off the boat and wait for Derrick. He follows me off the dock, and I can feel that joyful air about him is missing. When we reach the house, he follows me up the porch steps. He leans back against the wood siding and looks out ahead.

"Wanna come in for a few?" I ask him. I hate the idea of him leaving like this. Like the real Derrick has left his body. He looks at me for a moment, then the corner of his mouth tugs up. He nods, and I lead him inside. I grab us each a beer from the fridge—I figure he could definitely use one—and we walk out the back door to the deck. He puts the bottle to his lips, and I watch as he takes a swig of it, his brown eyes sparkling with the dimming sunlight. I turn and lean back against the railing before mustering up enough courage to ask him the question that's been burning on my mind.

"Has anything like that ever...ever happened to you?" I ask him, wrapping my arms around my body as I stand awkwardly next to him. He turns to face me, resting his arm on the railing.

"What, you mean like today?" he asks, that same half-smile creeping onto his lips. But I can't figure out what's funny about it. He looks down at the bottle in his hands and swirls it in circles. "Yeah, girl. Shit like that's happened to me before," he says just above a whisper. I narrow my eyes as they scour his face, wondering how anyone could ever see something dangerous about this man in front of me.

His gentle touch, the way he cares about his mom. The way he is with children, the fact that he's an intelligent business owner. But even if I didn't know all that, just his smile. The way he carries himself.

"How could anyone treat someone like you like that?" I whisper, and my eyes widen when I realize I've said it out loud. His eyes lift to mine, and he takes a tiny step closer to me. I swallow.

"This skin I'm in…" he whispers back. "Sometimes,

it feels like it may as well be a gun pointed in their face. Like it's a weapon."

I blink wildly, and I realize I'm fighting back tears. Tears of anger, of worry, of embarrassment of so much—my lack of understanding of what was happening. My blissful ignorance.

My mind flashes back to a conversation I had with Franklin. We were in the elevator, riding up to our floor, when another woman got in with us. She pulled herself to the front corner of the elevator and clutched her purse to her tight, tucking it under her arm.

When she got off, I mentioned it to Franklin. He gave me a sad smile and shrugged. We kept talking, and I never thought about it again. Not until right now.

"I can't even...I don't even know..." My voice trails off as I shake my head. "I should have said something else, done something else. I just didn't know—"

"You saw it today. And the truth is, you'll see something like that again," he says, coming even closer. I can smell the beer on his breath and whatever's left of that scent that drives me wild. "But now you know a little more. And the next time, you'll do a little more. It's what you *do* with that knowledge, Kaylee. And I know you'll do something."

"When you guys came in, Ryder..."

Derrick doesn't even need me to finish; he just nods.

"Ryder did the talking because it's usually a little safer that way," he says.

That skin will get you a lot of free passes in this world.

"You had to be so angry," I say. He nods, a chuckle escaping his mouth.

"So angry I could hit someone—like a convenience store owner," he says, and a chill runs through me. I've never seen this side of him. "But I can't act like I want to act in situations like that. Sometimes it literally means life or death. And you never know which card you're gonna draw."

My eyes lift to his, tears beading in their corners. I look down at his arms, the muscles flexed through his cut-off sleeves, the veins that crawl down his hands. I reach my finger out, tracing one of them from his hand up his wrist.

"This skin…" I whisper, doing the same with my other hand on his other arm. Chills pop up behind my fingers as I drag them up his arms. "It's so damn beautiful. How could anyone… It's so…*you* are so beautiful," I tell him, my eyes lifting back to his. When my hands reach his chest, he puts one of his on top of them, pressing them into him. With his other hand, he reaches out and cradles the back of my head, drawing me in closer. And then our lips crash together, fast and hard, like they've been waiting for this since the night we first laid eyes on each other.

I reach my hand up to cup the side of his cheek and wrap the other arm around his neck. The scent of him so up close makes me wild, and heat pools in my belly and down between my legs as I feel myself getting closer and closer to that line he was so sure we shouldn't cross.

But to my pleasant surprise, his arms wrap around me, and he lifts me off the ground, setting me on the railing. His tongue slips into my mouth once, and I open my eyes for a second to make sure it's all real. Mine moves to meet his, and my teeth tug at his bottom lip as we slowly come apart.

His eyes jump back and forth between mine, like he's looking for an answer to something that he thinks will be there. I can see him contemplating his next move, and the waiting is enough to drive me mad. I scoot closer to him so that our centers are touching, and I can feel the heat radiating off of his body. I lock one of my legs around his, pulling us even closer, and I can feel his hardness beneath his shorts. I let my hand slide up his arm, wrapping it around his neck. And then I pull him back in for another kiss, this time not letting him go until I get my point across.

I want him. I've wanted him below me, on top of me, any which way, since I saw him. Knowing nothing about him, I'd never felt a physical attraction like this. But now that I know him, I know some of his past, I know some of his pain, I want him *more*. I'm not sure if giving myself to him can cure some of that pain, can fix some of what's been broken, but I'd like to give it a try.

"Kaylee," he whispers between kisses as my lips leave his and take over on his jaw, ears, neck.

"Let me," I whisper back, taking his hand and placing it on my thigh. "Just let me tonight."

A fire ignites behind his eyes, and I can see that he's giving in. He wraps both hands around my thighs and pulls me onto him, lifting my ass off the railing. He kisses me again, harder this time, pushing me up against the cool glass of the door. He fiddles with the handle but can't get it open. He pulls away for a second, and we look around.

There's no one here.

The next house is a few hundred yards away, and you can't even see it through the pines that grow so thick together.

We have the same idea at the exact same time.

He carries me to one of the chaise lounges, setting

me down gently as ever. He stands back and pulls his shirt up over his head, and a bolt of electricity courses through my most sensitive spot. I need his hands on me. I need his hands *there*. I stare at him, his broad chest with that scar, the valleys of every muscle that make up the perfect man that stands in front of me. His dark-brown skin that makes me want him even more.

He reaches forward, tugging at the hem of my tank top, pulling it gently over my head. I unclasp my bra, and it slides down my arms. He pulls it off and takes me in, and I tuck my hair behind my ear subconsciously.

He leans forward, leaving one kiss on my collar bone. Then another, a little lower down. Then another, even lower, until he takes a nipple into his mouth, rolling it around on his tongue. I drop my head back, leaning back on my arms. I moan his name, and he lifts his head.

"What do you want, Kaylee?" he asks.

"You," I tell him, my voice husky and coarse. That half-smile tugs at his lips, sending me into overdrive. I reach for his waistband and pull him closer to me, letting my hand slip down beneath them and into his boxers. I take his length in my hand, stroking him gently at first then faster as he moves closer. He drops his head back, and I lick my lips at the sight of his Adam's apple bobbing in his thick neck.

He pushes me back gently and slips a hand down between us, into my jean shorts, then dips one finger under the lace of my thong. My panties are still a little damp from being thrown in the water earlier, but they're also damp now for another reason. And that reason is getting dangerously close to making me lose my complete mind.

He slips another finger down, then another, and his whole hand is in my panties. Before I can articulate the sheer ecstasy I'm feeling with his hands on me, he gently presses two fingers against my clit, massaging it in slow, deep circles. Then he picks up the pace, and I drop my hand from his dick to steady myself on either side of the chair. I slide back against the cushion, lying completely flat as he uses his other hand to unbutton and unzip and give himself more access. As he tugs my shorts down, he leaves a trail of kisses up the inside of my thigh, and I involuntarily moan his name. Then he pushes my legs apart and tugs my panties to one side before slipping a finger inside of me. My back arches as he reaches the deepest parts of me, then he adds another finger while his other hand continues with the circles. I've never hit the brink this quick before—not even with myself. He moves faster, his tongue tracing a line from my thigh to my very core.

And then I come undone in his hand, my body arching, and stiffening, then melting into a puddle in front of him. I'm panting, my eyes closed, as I lie back against the cushion, hand on my chest. He leaves gentle kisses just above my panty line, then my stomach, then my chest. And then I realize he's putting my panties back in place and tugging my shorts back up.

Wait.

This can't be over.

This. Can. Not. Be. Over.

I push myself up onto my elbows.

"What are you doing?" I ask, breathing like I just ran a marathon. He reaches down to shift and rearrange himself.

"I'm not gonna do this."

"Wha-what? Do what? In case you didn't notice, you already started." I'm still panting. My hair is slicked to my face. I'm *so* not ready for this to be over. But he shakes his head.

"I'm not just gonna fuck you out here on this deck and then leave."

Hearing the words "fuck you" come out of his mouth—and in the good sense—makes me want to lie back and throw my legs apart in front of him again.

"So don't go." A sly smile spreads across his lips.

"But what about tomorrow? The next time? What about when your dad calls and you gotta run back to run the empire?"

I sit in silence for a moment. I have no idea what to say. I just know what I feel in this moment, and that's that I need every inch of Derrick inside of me, wrapped around my body. If he just made me come that hard with his fucking *fingers*, I have to know what the rest of him can do to me. And I want to know what I can do to *him*. I want to take that pain he was feeling and turn it into the best damn pleasure he's ever had. I want to use my best moves, do whatever he wants until he feels whole again. But it feels like that reality is slowly fading away, so I straighten out my jeans and reach for my tank top. When I don't say anything, he kneels down in front of me.

"I told you, girl, that when I touch you, *really* touch you, I'm not gonna stop until I know every inch of you is satisfied."

"I'll believe that when I see it. You're sort of leaving me hangin'," I say. He chuckles as he pulls his shirt back on over his head.

"I can't, Kaylee. Not until you decide what it is you

want to do," he tells me. He kneels to kiss me one more time, then stands up. My lips tingle as he pulls away.

"Because you're worried you're in my head?"

He pauses at the back door and turns to me.

"No," he says. "Because you're in mine."

18

After the sexcapade that never was last night, I got almost no sleep. I rolled around in bed all night, tossing and turning, reliving the glorious, fleeting moments of his hands on me then feeling that same inevitable disappointment when they stopped.

I woke up from the little sleep I did get as the sun was rising this morning. I'm sitting on the front porch, lacing up my shoes. Maybe a long run will get rid of this lady boner that will not go away.

I turn down Joan's Way and pick up the pace as I find my footing on the side of the road. The sky is a dull purplish-gray color, untouched by the full force of the sun just yet. I breathe in and out, looking around at the tall trees. The lake is quiet this time of day, no boats to disrupt its serenity, no water skiers, no noise pollution. Just crystal-like water, sparkling beneath the earliest rays. The trees sway a bit in the early morning breeze, and chills ripple across my skin. There's something cooler, fresher, about these mountain summers.

As I round a bend in the road, I think about how

long I've been here. It's only been about a month, but it feels so much longer. And in the same breath, I still feel like I have so much to learn. And so much to decide.

One of those is how to deal with my parents. How to confront them on the fact that they've lied to me for almost my entire life. How to confront *her* on the fact that she abandoned a child. A child that's just as much hers as I am. How, because of them, I missed out on a grandmother who was seemingly a saint walking the earth. Who loved me despite all she missed.

Haven's words on the boat yesterday ring in my ear.

That skin. That skin will get you a lot of free passes in this world.

I look down at my forearms as they pump next to my sides.

Is this skin the reason I got to keep my mother?

I shake my head. The thought is too devastating, too despicable to even think about. It was because of the affair. That's it.

But as I run, suddenly, it becomes harder to breathe. I feel a lump in my throat. I feel it rising to the top, making my breaths shallow and sharp.

And then I can't breathe at all.

I pull off to the side of the road at the crest of a big hill, bending over and putting my hands on my knees. I'm wheezing, drawing in deep breaths—or at least trying to. I hear a car ahead and notice that it's getting closer. I scoot farther off to the side of the road, but I hear the brakes screech as the car stops in front of me.

"You good?" Haven asks, and I flick my eyes up to hers. She looks fine. She looks as effortlessly flawless as she has since I've known her, matter-of-factly going about her day like she wasn't traumatized yesterday. Like there was no chance she was the victim of racial profiling. Or maybe worse.

I nod slowly, raising myself up to stand.

"Just not used to these hills yet, I guess," I say. I walk toward the car and bend down into the open window. "What are you doing up so early?"

She shrugs.

"Didn't sleep well last night."

I bet.

"Where ya headed?"

"To May's, actually. I need to grab a few things. I was gonna try to sneak in and out

without waking you, but I guess I don't need to worry about that. You want a ride back?"

I turn back in the direction of the house. I've probably only run about a mile, but I'm just not feeling it today. I nod and hop in the passenger seat. We drive in silence for a few minutes before I turn to her.

"How are you, uh, feeling today? Ya know, just about...about…"

She smiles.

"About the racist prick who had his dick in a knot when he thought I stole some damn chips or something?" There's still a smile on her face, but I'm not sure how to react. It doesn't feel funny to me.

"Yeah, about that," I say. She shrugs as she rounds the last bend in the road before May's driveway. "I feel like...I feel like it's just one more reminder that no matter how hard you try, some people are still gonna not like you before they even know you."

She parks the car in the driveway and takes off her seatbelt.

"That was sorta how I was with you," she admits, and I drop my eyes to my lap.

"If I were you, I wouldn't like me either," I say. "Especially knowing who raised me."

"Nah." She shakes her head. "That's not fair. We don't have to become the people who raise us. And you haven't run off with millions, so maybe there's hope for you yet." She smiles again, and I reciprocate, swallowing nervously as she gets out of the car.

Yet.

We walk up the front porch, and I reach into my waistband for my key just as she puts hers in the door. She walks in ahead of me and makes her way up the stairs to her room. I go into the kitchen and pour myself a cup of water, scrolling through my phone. As I'm staring at the screen, a photo of my dad and me at our beach house flashes on my screen.

"Daddy" drags across the screen in big white letters, and I want to vomit. I stare down at it. I'm not ready. I don't know what I'm doing. I don't know anything.

"You busy right now?" Haven asks, and I jerk my head up to look at her.

"Uhh…" I say, fumbling to hit the "decline" button before going on. "No. Free as a bird."

"Cool. I'm gonna grab a few things and wait for you out here."

I nod and cock my head.

"Where are we going?" She smiles.

"I'm gonna show you around a little more. I know you had the Derrick Thomas tour, but I'm sure you were drooling a little too much to really take it all in." She chuckles to herself, and I scoff.

But after last night, I don't even care to hide it, at

least not with Haven, although I'm not sure why. I still don't know her. But maybe it's the way that she seems to know *me*. She seems to get me; she can read me.

She's not wrong, though. I haven't gone a minute without thinking about him since last night, and I'm pretty sure now I never will.

The way he looked at me, that fire in his eyes, the gentle but firm way his hands wrapped around me, the expertise with which his fingers...*ahem*. I jog up the steps and strip down in my room, hopping in the hot shower. I'm back down in just a few minutes, and Haven's sitting at the kitchen island, sorting through some mail. She stuffs a few of the envelopes in her bag and stands up.

"You ready?"

"Yep."

We walk back out the front door, and she locks it behind us, and I forget for a moment that this house is technically mine, too. She's so comfortable, so natural here.

We drive into town, and my stomach flips a little bit as we pass Big Moon Sports on our right. But she keeps driving and pulls into the little cafe that was next door to the convenience store where the *incident* occurred. I swallow as she puts the car in park. I look at her as she pulls the keys from the ignition.

"What?" she asks. I swallow again, my eyes darting toward the store. She looks up at it then lets out a long breath.

"I gotta keep living my life," she says. "If I'm scared, he wins. Come on."

I look up at the store again, my stomach swirling with a hot mix of anxiety and anger. I'm surprised at the way my body reacts, how my head is spinning with a replay of the events of yesterday. How I want to go back into that store, stand in front of Wayne, scream in his face. Stand between him and Haven. Cover her. *Protect* her.

The vision of Derrick's face, the rage in his eyes, hooded by an all-knowing look of a man who was trapped where he stood.

But I wasn't trapped. I've never been trapped—not in that way. Trapped by my family, maybe. By my parents. By their fortune. By the *destiny* they concocted before I was through grade school—best-in-the-state, private grade school, that is.

My breaths are heavy and labored, but I'm brought back down to earth when she taps on my window. I hop out and follow her into the small cafe. I'm hit with the life-saving scent of fresh-brewed coffee and some sort of cinnamon treat wafting toward me as we walk toward the front counter.

"Hey, Jules," Haven says, and I smile and nod.

"Hey, ladies," she says. "You're here early."

"Good thing you guys open at the crack of dawn." Haven smiles. "Coffee?" she asks me. I nod.

"Black, please," I say. Haven smiles.

"Two black coffees and two of the cinnamon buns, please," she says. Jules nods as Haven extends her credit card. I reach for my wallet, but she stops me.

"I got this one. I got some inheritance, too, remember?" she says with a smile. "I might not be able to use it just yet, but I'll keep a tab."

We grab our snacks and walk out the side door. Haven leads us to a table on a small patio that overlooks the water, and we sit down.

I pop a piece of the bun into my mouth and moan as it melts.

"Good, right?" she asks as she does the same. I nod, and we both look around. "Ya know, when they first opened, this patio wasn't here."

I look up at her.

"May lent them money to build it out a few years back, and they were able to increase their capacity. Increased their ROI by 250%."

"Wow."

"Yeah. Put the owner's kid through college," Haven says. I look back to the cafe.

"Jules?" She shakes her head.

"Nah, Jules is just working here to make ends meet. Her mom actually owns the bakery in town. She works both places, till she figures out what she's doing," she says. "The owners live down the road a bit. Been here for decades."

"What do you mean 'figures out what she's doing'?"

Haven claps her hands together and wipes them on a napkin.

"Jules has had it tough. She's sorta…lost, ya know? When they were kids, she lost one of her best friends up here. And then she sorta lost her *other* best friend as a result. Her parents aren't the most supportive, so aside from Derrick and Ryder and the rest of them, she is sorta on her own."

I look back through the window at Jules scrubbing away at a spot on the counter.

Although I've been spoon-fed anything I could possibly need, I'm starting to feel some sort of solidarity with Jules. *I'm on my own now.*

We finish up, throw away our trash, and hop back in her car.

After a few more minutes, she turns right up a steep road, and as we climb the mountain, my ears pop with the pressure. As we near the crest of the hill, there's a clearing in the trees, and I can see the lake shining through below. Dark, blackish blue, shimmering in the morning sunlight.

"Man, it really is stop-you-in-your-tracks beautiful up here," I say.

"Yeah," she says. "You'd think after being here my whole life, I wouldn't notice it as much. But damn if it doesn't make me stop every once in a while."

At the top of the mountain, she takes a right and drives a little ways before she pulls into a gravel parking lot. A small building sits toward the back, and a turquoise sign reads *Peake Gifts*. As we walk through the door, a bell chimes above us. A piccolo plays over the sound system above us, and some sort of incense is burning toward the back of the store. There are big, beautiful paintings on every wall, Native American men and women in them dancing, making pottery, hunting.

Glass counters line the walls of the store, filled with beautiful turquoise jewelry and pendants.

"Hey, lady," I hear a familiar voice call from behind me.

"Luna, hey," I say.

"What are you doing here?"

"I thought I'd give her more of a tour," Haven says from behind me. "Wanted to show her all the gems of Meade Lake. This here is Luna's family's shop."

I nod and look around.

"It's awesome. This stuff is gorgeous," I say, pointing

to the jewelry. Luna smiles as she walks behind the counter.

"My mom makes most of it," she says with pride in her eyes. She unlocks one of the sections and pulls out a mat with a bracelet and matching earrings.

"She *makes* these?" I ask. Luna smiles and nods.

"Yep. Just like my grandmother, and great-grand-mother, and great-great-grandmother did before her. I haven't got it down yet, so I just stand here and sell them."

I pick one of the earrings up from the mat and twirl it around in my fingers.

"I'll take the set," I tell her. Her eyes light up.

"Really?" she asks. I get the impression from the sparse lot and empty shop that there's not a ton of traffic up here on the mountain.

"Yes, please," I tell her. She takes the earring from me and walks toward the register to wrap them up in paper. As she's ringing me up, I see another bracelet similar to the one I'm buying. "I'll take that one, too." She gives me a look but hurriedly grabs the other one and adds it to my bag.

"This is a really incredible shop," I tell her again. She smiles as she looks around.

"This shop is pretty much all my family has left. This shop and this side of the mountain," she says, her eyes trailing out the window to her left. I want to ask what she means, but Haven rounds the corner behind us.

"You ready to go?" I hold up my bag and nod.

"Yep," I say. "Thanks again, Luna."

We get back in and pull our seat belts on, and Haven turns back onto the main road.

"That place was adorable," I say. Haven nods.

"Yeah. It used to be one of the more popular shops in Meade Lake," she says. "They developed the mountain so much that it's pretty much all houses up here aside from the Peake's half. They own this side of the mountain."

"They own it?" I ask. She nods.

"Yeah. Luna's mom is Shawnee. There's record of her ancestors living on this land as far back as the 1400s."

"Damn," I say.

"But over time, as we always seem to do in this country, they were pushed out. Forced to move, forced to change. And her family lost everything they once had to resorts and vacation homes. So they cling to the land they do have pretty fiercely."

I nod.

"Wow. That's quite the burden to bear."

"It is," she says. "The shop doesn't bring in the revenue it used to, either. Gran May lent them money a few times, too."

When we get to the bottom of the mountain, Haven makes a few more turns, and I realize we're headed to Alma's.

"Mind if we stop by Alma's? I know she wanted to see you," Haven says.

"Sure thing," I say. There's something so soothing about Alma's presence that I feel almost giddy about seeing her.

We pull into her driveway, and I see Mila's car parked next to the house. To my disappointment, I don't see Derrick's truck.

"Hi, babies," Alma calls to us from the living room. When we walk in, we see Mila standing up on a stool, a beautiful ivory gown hanging off of her body and flowing to the floor. Alma is on her knees in front of her, pins between her teeth, sticking them in strategically.

"Wow," I say, "that dress is stunning." Mila smiles as she looks down at it.

"Thanks," she says. "I can't believe I'm getting married in six days." Then her eyes dart to me as she gasps. "Oh, shit. Kaylee!"

"What?" I ask.

"The wedding! I didn't even think to tell you about it. You weren't here when we sent out the invites, and we weren't sure how long you'd—oh, my gosh. I'm so embarrassed. Will you come? Please?"

"Hold still, girl," Alma calls from below, and Mila quickly snaps back to attention.

"Oh, gosh, Mila," I say, "you don't have to do that. Seriously."

She waves a hand at me.

"Hold *still*, girl!" Alma says again, and Mila makes a face. I giggle.

"Please. It would mean so much! Especially with May not being here. I mean, not that you'd be replacing her or anything, just that—" She pauses mid-sentence, likely to try to pull the foot from her mouth.

"You should come," Haven says from behind me, sipping water from a glass.

Knowing she wants me there, knowing that she doesn't feel like I'm impeding on her life, makes me want to go.

"You should, baby," Alma agrees, pushing up from the ground to look at the back of the dress. "Be with everyone at a happy occasion. It'll be a nice change of pace. Plus, you can see how the Meade Lake crew puts on a party."

"Yeah, buddy!" Mila says, pumping her arms in the air and doing an insanely uncoordinated dance. Alma shoots her a look that could absolutely kill, and she freezes again.

After Alma puts the last of the pins and the basting into the dress, she helps Mila out of it, and we all have lunch on the back deck. We spend the afternoon laughing, looking at old photo albums, telling stories, and soaking in the mountain air. Before I know it, we're having dinner, too, and the sun is going down behind the mountains behind us. Life here is a little slower, a little quieter, but a hell of a lot more peaceful.

I think I'm getting used to it.

My eyes grow wide at the thought. Because this life isn't mine. At least, it's not the one I'm supposed to have. It's not the life that 204 people rely on me for.

"You want me to take you back?" Haven asks, and I shake my head, clearing all thoughts of my *other* life—my *real* life—from my head.

"Oh, yeah, thanks," I say, standing up to clear my dishes. I hug Alma and Mila and type the details of the wedding into my phone, promising her I'll be there.

When Haven pulls into May's driveway, I unbuckle slowly. I reach down for the bag I got from Luna's store and pull out one of the bracelets.

"I, uh, I got you this," I tell her. Her eyes grow into saucers. I hold it out to her then pull the other one out. She looks at the two bracelets then back to me. A small smile pulls the corner of her mouth up.

"What?" I ask.

"Nothin'," she says, taking it and clasping it around

her wrist. "Just that, a month ago, I didn't think I'd ever have a sister. Now, I have a sister I have matching friendship bracelets with. Life's crazy like that." I smile back at her. "Thank you."

When I get inside the big old house, I collapse onto the couch. And as I do, I feel my phone vibrate in my back pocket. When Derrick's name flashes before my eyes, I jump up. We haven't spoken since last night when he pushed me to the most pleasure I've ever had with a man—and that's really saying something, considering we didn't even have sex.

"Hello?" I ask, barely letting it ring once.

"I hear you're going to a wedding this weekend," he says. I bite my bottom lip.

"I am," I say.

"What a coincidence. I happen to be in need of a date to the same wedding." I can't fight the idiotic smile that's crossing my lips.

"Oh, is that so?"

"It is. What do ya say?"

"I mean, I have *so* many suitors calling," I say with a chuckle. "But I guess I can move you to the top of the list." He laughs on the other end, and it sends my hormones into overdrive.

"I'd be so appreciative. I'll pick you up at four?"

"Sounds perfect." We hang up, and I flop back onto the couch like a teenager who just had her first kiss. As I lie back, my phone vibrates again. I hop back up, expecting it to be him again. Only, it's not. It's a text from my mother.

I know you're not in Miami. Open the door.

Shit.

19

My heart is beating in my throat. I'm afraid to even turn to look out the front door. I'm not ready for this. I'm not ready for her. I don't have my bearings together. I have so much I need to say to her, so many questions to ask her, so much to scream, so many tears to cry. But right now, I don't want to say a word. I want to turn all the lights off and pretend no one's home. But it's too late. I hear the rap of her knuckles on the glass door.

I swallow as I pull myself off the couch and down the hall into the foyer. I can see her standing on the porch, looking around. Her hair is darker than mine, a dark brown compared to my honey-blonde waves, but everyone always said our faces looked the same. I used to love that. Now, I'm not so sure. Her perfectly colored locks are pulled back into a bun, and she's wearing a designer blouse and heels. I almost want to laugh. Leave it to Karnie Jennings, Georgia's number-one trophy wife, to always, *always* play the part.

She turns toward the door, and our eyes meet

through the glass. I open it slowly, and a cold breeze blows between us, chills rippling on my skin. She takes a step toward me, but I step out onto the porch, pulling the door shut behind me.

This isn't her house. And something about her being here feels so, so wrong. Her eyes are wide as she looks me up and down.

She lets out a long sigh then wraps her arms around me, pulling me into her. I can't bring myself to lift my arms. Not even the slightest bit. She steps back when she feels how stiff the embrace is and looks at me.

"How did you know I was here? What are you doing here?" I ask her. A defensive look passes over her face as she leans back on her hip, crossing her arms over her chest.

"I could ask you the same thing," she says. "Your pal Emma spilled the beans on you to her dad. This place looks exactly the same," she adds, looking up and down at the house. *Fucking Emma. I should have known.* She looks behind me through the door. "Where is she? Is she here?"

My heart rate starts to accelerate.

She wants to know about Haven. My sister. Her daughter. She's here for her. And I'm not sure if I should be overjoyed, welcome her change of heart, or be jumping in front of Haven the way I wanted to with Wayne that day at the store.

"No. She's not staying here right now," I say. "But I can see about you meeting her. She's pretty incredible, Mom. I actually think she...I actually think she looks like you a little bit."

Her eyes grow wide, and she tilts her head to one side the slightest bit.

"I meant May," she says, her voice low and strained. I tilt my head back slowly. "I don't

know what she's told you. She shouldn't have said a damn word. She swore she'd never—"

"May is dead."

She stops, her hands dropping to her side, her eyes blinking uncontrollably. I don't know how to react. The part of me that was raised by her, nurtured by her, *loved* by her, wants to reach out and hold her. Understand the immense pain of losing a mother.

But the part of me that was born here in Meade Lake, just a few weeks ago, is realizing that I'm losing a mother, too.

She's not here to meet her other daughter. She's here to take one back.

"Oh."

Oh?

"But *Haven* is here in Meade Lake. Alive and well."

Her eye twitches as she stares at me, her jaw shaking with what looks to be rage.

"Kaylee, you need to come home now. This has gone on long enough. Nothing good can

come from you being here."

I cross my arms over my chest.

"Actually, a lot of good has come over the last few weeks. A lot of truths."

She narrows her eyes at me.

This isn't the daughter she's used to. She's used to me being like her. She's used to me

"yes, ma'am"-ing. She's used to me going along with every idea she or my father had. Every plan they had for me.

"Enough. We can talk about this later. But you need

to come home. We need you to sign the paperwork for the women-owned status. Things are getting tighter. It's time to come home and stop playing around up here. Your father needs—"

I feel a fire coursing through my veins, an anger like I've never felt.

"Do you want to meet her, Mom?" I ask, my voice quiet and quivering with fury. Her mouth snaps shut, her eyes boring into mine. I narrow mine as tears rise to the brim. She breaks our staring match and looks down at the ground, rubbing her temple with her perfectly manicured nails.

"Kaylee, the past is the past. It's done, and nothing can be undone. Now, I'm sorry to hear about your grandmother—"

"'My grandmother?' Do you mean *your* mother?" I ask, my voice getting louder now.

She swallows audibly, and I want to scream. She still doesn't say anything. She doesn't acknowledge my words. She doesn't acknowledge May or Haven.

"I came here to let you know that the business is in trouble. There are more layoffs—"

"She's gorgeous, Mom. She's tall and has these beautiful, big brown eyes. She's smart, too. Studying business at Sinclair. She's—"

"Kaylee," my mother tries to cut in. But I refuse. Haven's been ignored for so long. Not anymore.

"She's funny, too. She has this real sarcastic tone. I guess she gets that from May. But I wouldn't know."

"Enough!" my mother shouts, and I'm breathing so heavily that my chest is heaving up and down. "I came here to tell you to stop playing around up here! We're on the brink of losing everything. *Everything.* And you're up here playing around. And on whose dime, Kaylee? It's time to put this little adventurous, self-righteous phase to bed and get your ass back to Georgia."

She shrinks back a bit when she's done, realizing the weight of what she's said. The words "fuck you" are flashing through my brain, but strangely, I feel calm and cool. I feel clarity.

"You need to leave."

She scoffs, crossing her arms back over her chest.

"*Excuse* me?"

"You heard me. Get off my porch."

"*Your* porch?" she asks. I nod.

"*My* porch. Go."

"Who the *fuck* do you think you're talking to?" she asks, her voice growing louder. She's not used to losing, not when what she wants is also what my father wants. I know there's a reason she's here by herself. And it's because this—me, May, Haven—is *her* problem. A problem she was supposed to have fixed when I was five. I take a step closer to her, and she shrinks back again.

"Get the hell off my porch. Do us both a favor, Mom, and leave us *both* this time."

Her lip is quivering, and I can see her eyes are glossy with tears. But there's no fiber of me left to feel anything but disdain toward her. Not an inch of me that wants to reach out anymore. She's not mourning her dead mother or the relationship she never had with the daughter she abandoned. She's mourning life as she knew it, with her blonde-haired, blue-eyed daughter to play a critical role.

She stays frozen in her spot, and I see her mouth opening to speak.

"I think you need to leave, ma'am," I hear Derrick say, and I suddenly feel strong, sturdy.

She turns to him slowly, her eyes widening as he makes his way up the porch steps. He takes his position next to me, and I let out a breath. I don't take my eyes off of her.

Her eyes narrow at him and flick back to me.

"This isn't over. We *will* talk about this more," she says before slinking off the porch and clicking back to her Mercedes. I stand perfectly still as she slams the door shut then peels out of the driveway.

And when nothing is left but dust in her trail, I sink back against the house, cover my mouth, and start to sob. I could feel it coming; I felt the crumbling of the woman I *thought* was my mother, right before my eyes. But it doesn't make it any easier. Because now I'm mourning the mom I thought I knew.

"Hey, hey," he says, kneeling next to me. I bury my face into his chest and let him wrap his hard body around me. I feel every word my mother said, every moment she spent avoiding the subject of Haven burning on my skin.

"How can *that* be the woman that raised me? How can she be so fucking heartless?" I cry as I sink down on the ground. He scoots closer to me, pulling me into him tighter. "She didn't even blink when I told her May was dead. Her *mother*. And she has another child, a daughter that's still alive, and she won't even say her name. She won't even acknowledge her existence. What does that say? And if you never came down, I would have never known any of this. I would have lived the rest of my life thinking they were as perfect as I...as I was trained to believe. I would have lived the rest of my life without knowing a single thing about May. Without knowing Haven existed, just like they wanted."

My eyes lift up to his.

"I would have lived the rest of my life without knowing you."

His eyes drop to my hands, and he picks one up, bringing it to his lips.

"I can't imagine life without knowing you," he whispers. His eyes find mine again, and I stare at every inch of his beautiful face. The big brown eyes drilling into me, seeing me like no other eyes ever have.

"I could have ended up just like her," I whisper. He moves so that he's directly in front of me and takes my face in his hands.

"Look at me," he says. I do. "Whether or not you knew about any of this, any of us, you would never, *ever* be like her. You're too good, too beautiful, to ever be like that. No matter where you ended up."

I look up at him, my lip quivering. He strokes my cheeks with his thumbs then pulls my lips to his, letting them land gently at first. He pulls away for a moment, looking into my eyes with an intensity that makes my whole body shake.

"You're too beautiful," he whispers again before pulling me back in for another kiss, this time with much more urgency. His lips scour mine, his tongue finding its way between mine, making me push up onto my knees. I wrap my arms around his neck, and he wraps his arms under my legs, pushing himself up to stand. He kisses me again, opening the front door and kicking it closed behind us. We move slowly at first as he shifts me around to his front, letting my legs wrap around his waist. When I feel how hard he is, desire shoots through me like a lightning bolt. I move my hips, pressing against him and making him moan. He pulls apart, staring at me for a minute.

"Is this going to be one of those stop-in-the-middle things?" I ask. A half-smile creeps onto his lips, but the rest of his face remains serious as he scans mine. He shakes his head.

"Not tonight, girl," he says just above a whisper. "I couldn't stop if I tried." He carries me toward the steps, taking them two-by-two, kissing my lips, my jaw, my neck.

He walks to my room and gently lays me on the bed, crawling on top of me and holding my face in place as he devours my mouth again. My body arches underneath him, the spot between my legs pulling toward him like he has a gravitational pull on it.

"I told you, girl," he says, sliding his lips to my neck then to my collar bone. "I'm gonna take my time. Just like you deserve."

I shiver at the thought, closing my eyes and waiting for him to bring to life the exact fantasy I've been having for more than a month. He steps down from the bed and reaches for the hem of my shirt, pulling it swiftly up over my head. He lets his hands trail down to my jean shorts and unfastens them, letting them slip off my legs onto the floor. He lifts one of my legs, leaving a gentle kiss on the top of my foot then trailing up to my ankle, my calf, and the back of my knee. I close my eyes and try to steady my breathing, soaking in every mark he's leaving on my body. He gets to my thigh and gently pushes my legs wider apart. I can feel the wetness; I can feel what he's doing to me as he gets closer. He kisses the inside of one thigh, letting his fingers dance up the other.

I moan, and his eyes flick up to me. A devilish grin lights up his face.

"Girl, you ain't seen nothin' yet," he says. "Hold on."

His tongue wets the inside of my thigh, then I feel his finger slip in from the side of my panties. He gently strokes the outside of my folds, like he's giving me a moment to prepare for what's coming. I arch my back again, and he reaches up and slips a hand underneath my bra. He tugs at my nipple just as he slips two fingers inside of me, the sensation sending me into overdrive.

"Mmm," he moans as he feels around inside of me. I can feel my wetness dripping onto his fingers. "Is this for me, baby?"

I nod as I claw for the covers, pressing my head back into the mattress. Suddenly, his fingers slow down, and my eyes shoot open.

"Kaylee," he whispers, and my eyes meet his. "Is this all for me?" I nod again.

"Yes," I moan, "it's all for you. You did this to me."

"Did I?" he asks, kneeling down so that I can feel his breath on my pussy. I buck my hips in his direction.

"Yes," I say. "You've been doing this to me."

One of his eyebrows shoots up.

"Have I?"

He's playing with me, teasing me, now.

"Yes," I moan again.

"And what have you been doing about it, Kaylee?" I buck my hips in his direction again, my hand sliding down my navel and into my panties.

"Nothing compared to what you're doing now," I

whisper, and I gently massage my clit. His eyes light up in front of me. He pulls my panties to the side and kneels even closer.

"I told you, baby," he says. "You ain't seen nothin' yet."

His tongue laps up the length of my pussy, then again, then again, and I spread my legs wide for him, wanting him to devour me whole. He pushes a finger into me at the same time, and I can't feel any of my extremities. It's like every nerve ending, every pleasure receptor I have has gone between my legs.

"Derrick," I groan, pounding my hands into the bed. I reach down and push my fingers through his thick curls, pushing his head into me, wanting him to stay there forever. He kisses me, sucks me, tugs me in ways I didn't know were even possible, and my legs start to tremble.

"Derrick," I say again, but this time, it's a warning. He takes his hand from my breast and slides it down under my ass. He lifts me slightly off the bed.

"Not yet," he says between kisses of my softest spot. "I'm not done here."

I squirm beneath his lips, unsure of how much more I can take before I erupt.

He kisses me again, his fingers still dancing inside of me, then tilts me up just the slightest, and suddenly, I'm seeing stars. The new angle he's found is making it impossible for me to keep any sort of control of my own body. I'm his now, coming undone on his lips, losing myself in his hands.

"Derrick..." I gasp.

"Now, baby," he says, his fingers pumping in and out of me as his tongue finds my clit. And then I'm done. I explode, tugging his hair, digging my nails into his shoulders.

He slinks back slowly to his feet then reaches up and unhooks my bra, tugging it off my arms. I let my legs fall to the sides as I push myself up onto my elbows. He stands and pulls at his waistband, his eyes drilling into mine. I'm in complete awe of him and what he's just done. How he could read my body, plan every move, every flick of the tongue, every stroke of the finger, so that I was completely and utterly satisfied. And as my eyes watch as his pants drop to the ground, I know we're just getting started. He springs free from his boxers, and I suddenly forgot I just had the most explosive orgasm of my life. I'm ravenous; I need him. Every single inch of him. And from the looks of it, he has quite a few inches to give.

I scoot closer to the edge of the bed and reach out for him, taking his impressive length in my hand, pumping my hand up and down, watching as his head drops back. I reach up and pull his lips to mine, turning him and pushing him onto the bed. I hop off and kneel in front of him, eyeing his dick like it's a forbidden fruit. I slide my hand up and down one more time then pull him into my mouth, savoring his taste. I move up and down, and with every groan that escapes his lips, I'm hungry for more. Finally, I let him fall from my mouth, our eyes meeting again. I crawl up his body, my legs straddling him. When our lips meet again, he flips me onto my back. He kneels down to his shorts, grabbing a condom from his wallet and tearing it open with his teeth.

"You ready, baby?" he asks me. Every time he calls

me that, I melt a little more. I pull my legs wider apart and let my tongue wet my lips.

"Yes," I whisper. His solid chest heaves as he rolls it on, then he pulls me to the edge of the bed. He lifts my legs up to wrap around his waist then slowly pushes himself into me. I notice his length even inside of me, and I clench my muscles to take him further and further in.

"You okay?" he asks. I nod, wrapping my legs around him tighter and pulling him down for another kiss.

"Let me have you," I whisper.

"You got me, girl," he says then pushes in further, picking up the pace as he moves in and out of me. I wrap my arms around his neck, pulling him close to me, kissing his neck and his ear.

"Kaylee," he whispers, his grip around my waist getting tighter.

"Mmm?"

"You got me," he says again, our eyes meeting for the briefest moment. And I don't think he means I have him in the sense that he's inside of me right now. I think he means it more than that. He plunges into me again, harder and faster, until we're both panting and saying each other's names in unison.

"Yes, Derrick, please," I whimper beneath him. He pounds into me again, once more, twice more, and then he lets out one last groan as he bows his head, a shudder going through his body. I feel him shudder inside me as I come again, my legs dropping like dead weight on either side of him. He presses his forehead to mine for a few moments, letting us both catch our breath. He slips off the bed and into the bathroom then returns in a moment's time and lifts the covers. He wraps his hand around my bicep and tugs me up toward him, pulling the comforter down over both of us. He pulls me into his chest, leaning down for another kiss. When we come apart, he looks into my eyes, stroking the side of my cheek with his thumb again.

I've had one-night stands before; I've had random hookups; I've even had relationships. But never have I ever had someone look at me the way he's looking at me right now.

"You weren't kidding," I finally tell him, making him laugh. "I wish we hadn't waited all this time if *that's* what I was missing out on." He smiles again, tucking a piece of hair behind my ear. "Can I ask you a question?"

"Sure," he says, fluffing his pillow up underneath his head a bit. "What was different about tonight?" I ask him. "What made you stay tonight?"

He covers my hand with his, intertwining our fingers.

"I realized that I would rather only have you for a night than never have you at all."

He wraps his arm around my body tighter, pulling me into him closer, the heat of our bodies making my skin dewy.

I don't know what to say, how to respond. Because I know the truth is that I needed what he gave me as much as he needed to give it to me. I needed *him*. Maybe I still do.

I draw circles across his chest with my finger, trying to think of what to say. How to tell him that, in a little over a month's time, he's changed my entire life. How to tell him that I'm terrified of what the next week, month, *year* of my life holds. How I'm worried that it can't hold *him*. I think about what my mother said.

The business is in trouble.

Yeah, my parents might suffer if I don't take over and sign that venture. But so could 204 other people. People who work hard and devote the best hours of their week to that company. People like Franklin.

I shake my head. I can't think about it right now. Not when I'm basking in the glory of what just happened in this bed.

My finger lands on the scar that sits at the top of the right side of Derrick's chest, and I want to know what it's from. What—*who* hurt him like this. I want to know who could possibly cause this beautiful man any sort of pain. With his heart so big and pure and full of good intentions. I push myself up and kiss it over and over. I look up to ask him what it's from, but I realize his eyes are closed, his breathing slow and steady.

He's totally peaceful, and suddenly, so am I.

20

I roll over to feel for him only to find an empty spot on his side of the bed.

His side of the bed.

Just a mere month ago, this wasn't even *my* bed. And now, I want to share it with him.

I push up, pulling the sheets to my chest when I realize I'm still naked, and wonder for a

moment if last night really happened.

Every touch. Every taste. Every glorious minute. I look across the room at myself in the mirror and see the light-pinkish-brownish mark he left on my chest, and I smile.

Yep, it happened, alright.

But where is he now?

I head for the stairs, but I catch a glimpse of something out the door to my balcony. My heart stops at the sight of him, staring out over the water, the early glow of dawn making him look almost angelic. He's shirtless, his arms on either side of him, hands resting on the wood railing of the deck. I tiptoe to the door, taking in the view, my eyes trailing across every ripple of his back muscles, the broad shoulders that lifted me up so easily last night, the triceps I dug my nails into for dear life while he went to work on me. A chill shoots down to my middle as I lean my head against the door jamb, but the wood creaks beneath my feet, and he turns to look at me.

"Hey, you," he says with a smile. He holds a hand out, and I step out closer to him. "I was gonna come back to bed before you woke up so you wouldn't wake up alone."

I'm melting. I swear.

"As long as you didn't go too far," I say. "What are you doing out here?" He turns back to the water.

"Just looking. May always had the best views from this house. I like to wake up when Meade Lake does." I smile, and he pulls me into him and kisses my forehead. I tilt my head up, our eyes finding each other like magnets. He bends down for a kiss, and it's better than coffee first thing in the morning. I pull the covers tighter around me, and his eyes drop down to my body.

"That looks better on you than it does on the bed," he says, kissing my cheek. "Although, it'd probably look better off."

I giggle and turn into him, nuzzling up against him.

"Easy, tiger," I say. "I'm still trying to figure out if last night was real or not."

He turns me so that we're facing each other and cups my face in his hands. He clasps them around my head and pulls me in for another kiss. This time, a deeper, longer one. More like the ones he gave me last night.

"Last night was very real," he whispers as we come

apart. I open my eyes slowly, not wanting the moment to fade away. "I was gonna go for another run. You down?" I give him a devilish smile.

"You just want to take *all* my energy, don't you?" I ask. He gives me a sly grin back as he reaches around to cup my ass, pressing me into him.

"You have no idea," he says, biting his bottom lip as he looks me up and down again. "Come on, before you make me take you back in there."

I raise my eyebrows at him.

"Maybe that was my plan."

I let go of the sheet with one hand, letting it fall from my body, then turn on my heel to walk back into my room. He trails behind me, though, grabbing a hold of my wrist and pulling me back toward him so that he's pressing against my back. And I can feel how hard he is, his length brushing against my bare back. He slides one hand around my neck, turning my head toward him so he can kiss me, while the other slides down my navel, resting just on top of the spot he so professionally dominated just hours before. I moan as our lips find each other again, getting their bearings, reclaiming their space.

"Girl," he whispers, "I could do this all day."

"Then do it," I tell him, spinning to face him and throwing my arms around his neck. Before I even realize it, he's lifted me up, my legs wrapping around him like they've now been trained to do. He pushes me up against the door, the glass cool against my skin. He lunges for my neck, my lips, my face, one of his hands sliding up my back and tangling itself in my hair while the other slides between us, dipping into my most sensitive spot to see just how ready I am. And as I'm sure he can tell, I'm *ready*. I take hold of his bottom lip with my teeth, gently tugging on it as we pull apart.

"How do you do this to me?" he asks with that same mischievous half-smile that makes my whole body tingle. With one quick move, he grabs another condom from the pocket of his shorts then pushes them down below his ass. He tears it open between his teeth and uses his leg to balance my weight while he rolls it on. And before I have another second to say his name, he's inside me again, pushing me back against the glass harder, breathing into my neck and hair, one hand holding me up while the other slaps against the glass behind me.

He thrusts in and out, my back sliding up and down on the door. The combination of his intoxicating scent, the early morning glow around us, the quiet, sparkling water in the distance, brings me to the brink quickly.

"Harder, Derrick," I groan, kissing and biting his shoulder. "*Harder.*"

He groans as he picks up the pace, holding me steady while he moves faster, deeper. I scream out when he reaches down with his other hand to massage my clit, and then I'm there. Right on the edge and then over it. He comes just after I do, growling my name as his head drops to mine. Finally, he steps back and lets me slide down, pulling my face into his for another kiss. When we pull apart, he stares down at me, his eyes moving back and forth between mine. His thumbs stroke my cheeks, his fingers twining through my hair. With every glance, I feel a piece of my past chipping away, floating into the air, losing some of its meaning. Every second that passes in his grasp, I know that where I come from doesn't matter so much. The girl I used to be was missing some-thing. And the longer I let myself get lost in his golden-brown eyes, the more I realize that I might be finding it here. And it's equal parts beautiful and terrifying. Before, I had the blueprint for what my life would look like. Only, I wasn't the one laying any of the foundation.

Here, I'm starting with the paper and pencil in my own hand.

I kind of like that.

My heart is broken over the exchange with my mother last night. Over the idea of never really seeing my father again.

But when I look at Derrick, I think it can get better.

I think I can heal here.

A smile flashes over his lips again.

"What are you doin' to me, girl?" he asks. I smile back and shrug.

"I think the same thing you're doing to me," I tell him.

We go back into the house and clean up some then go downstairs and make some coffee.

"I need to swing by Mama's and help set up the arbor for the wedding," he says. "You wanna come?"

"Sure," I say, putting my mug in the sink and rinsing it out. I pause for a moment. "Do you think she'll...do you think they'll be able to...tell?"

"Tell what? That I've had you twice in the last twelve hours?"

I bite my lip and nod.

"Yeah. That." He thinks for a minute then laughs.

"Honestly, yeah," he says. "Just don't look anyone in the eye," he jokes.

· · ·

When we get to Alma's, there are a few cars in the driveway, and there's some buzzing going on around back. In the backyard, Teddy is taking directions from Camille on where to set up tables and chairs. Mila, Luna, and Jules are on either side of the aisle they've set up down the center of Alma's yard, placing flowers a few feet apart to line it. Ryder is sitting at a table by himself, his eyes pointed toward the trees.

"Hey, y'all," Derrick calls out as we walk around. Everyone gives us a quick "hi" then seems to do a double-take when they realize we're arriving together. I clear my throat nervously, but Derrick just nudges me and keeps walking toward Ryder.

"What are you doin'?" he asks him when we get closer.

"Nothing. Can't ya see? I'm sitting here like a fucking invalid," Ryder says, his voice gruff and cold. Derrick pulls a chair up and sets it directly in front of Ryder, spinning it around and sitting on it backwards.

"Look here, ya ass," he says, and even though I know he can't see him clearly, Ryder's eyes land right on him. "Two days from now, you're going to have the best day of your life. And that woman over there is about to have hers, too. You know what you need to see? Her. And Annabelle. And guess what? You already do. I know you know their faces like the back of your own damn hand. You know how beautiful she's gonna be without having to see her. And all she will see on that day is you. The flowers and the fucking chairs and centerpieces? Let her have that. You know I got you. It'll be just what she wants. And if you remember what that day means, it'll be just what you want, too. She's not marrying you for your eyes, you jackass. She's marrying you because, for *some* reason, she loves you."

A slow smile spreads across Ryder's face, and he reaches out to punch Derrick playfully in the arm.

"Good thing you're such a fucking giant," Ryder says, "or I might not have landed that punch." Derrick laughs, and Ryder's face grows more serious. "Thank you, man."

Derrick puts his hand on his shoulder then turns back toward the ladies to take some direction. I look after him, and Ryder does, too.

"You know when I lost my sight, he rebuilt our entire dock?" he asks. I turn to him.

"What?"

"He built a railing from the house to the water so that I can get down there safely on my

own. Sometimes, this shit," he says, motioning to his eyes, "can make ya feel less than human. Being able to get to the boat on my own gave me a little of that back."

I turn back to Derrick, watching him play around with Luna and Mila and Jules while also lifting entire tables with ease and moving them to their appointed spots.

"They don't make friends like him anymore," he says. "Shit. They don't make *family* like him anymore. Stick around for him, would ya?" he asks with a playful tone, but I can feel a little weight behind his words. I'm not sure how to respond, so I put my hand on his shoulder.

"I'm really happy for you, Ryder," I tell him, diverting. "You and Mila seem like you were created to find each other."

He smiles as he turns toward the direction of her laugh, closing his eyes as he basks in it.

"She's my north star, that woman. Everything makes sense when I turn toward her." I look at Derrick again, our eyes meeting from across the lawn. He winks at me, and I wink in return.

I think I know what you mean, Ryder.

I walk up the lawn and into the house to find Alma and say hello, but when I find her, she's frantically moving from pot to pot at the stove then turning around to chop onions on the island behind her. She has a towel thrown over her shoulder, and there's flour on her chin.

"Alma?" I ask. "My goodness, you're busy in here. Can I help?"

Her eyes flick up to me, and she freezes for a moment. She takes the towel off her shoulder and puts it down.

"Hey, baby," she says. "I heard you had a visitor last night." My eyes widen.

Oh, God. She knows. She can tell. She knows her son did dirty, dirty things to me not even an hour ago. She can tell.

"I, uh…"

"I heard your mother was in town."

Oh, shit. I almost completely forgot for a brief moment that I had seen my mother. That I had basically forced her to leave. That I excommunicated myself.

"Yeah, she did," I tell her.

"And how did that go?" Alma asks, her eyes like saucers.

"I told her…I told her to leave," I say, grabbing onto my arm with my other hand. "She didn't…she didn't even want to hear about Haven. She didn't even blink when I told her May died. I don't...I don't understand..."

My voice trails off as the pain of last night sets in. Derrick had been a good distraction, but I remember now. I remember the finality of what happened last night. Alma drops her head and shakes it once.

"Haven saw her," she says, her voice low. My eyes widen, my breath quickening.

"Wha...what?"

"I guess when she was leaving town last night, she stopped at the cafe beforehand. She looked right at her; they made eye contact. But she didn't say one word to Haven. Didn't even stay to get her coffee. She just...she just left."

I swallow what feels like a knife in my throat.

"Where is she?" I ask. Alma nods her head down the hallway.

"Hasn't come out of her room all day. I think she's pretty torn up about it. She really needs someone, but I just...I'm up to my elbows in this. I've got seventy-five people coming here in two days for this wedding, and I'm nowhere near ready."

I think for a minute. I might be the last person Haven wants to talk to right now. Especially when it deals with our mother. But I also might be her only choice.

"Do you...do you think I can try to talk to her?" I ask. Alma thinks for a moment and nods.

"Yeah, honey. Go ahead."

I walk down the hallway and follow Alma's directions, knocking on the last door on the left.

"Yeah?" Haven's quiet, cracking voice answers, and I push on the wood gently.

"Hey," I say. She's perched on a chair in the corner of the room, looking out of her window. She turns to me.

"Hey," she says. There's a long, awkward pause.

"You wanna get out of here?" I ask her. She narrows her eyes at me, skeptical. She looks out the window again at everyone laughing, getting ready for a celebration, and I know she doesn't feel much like celebrating. Finally, she turns to me and nods.

She gives me her keys, and I decide to make our first stop the snow cone shop Derrick took me to on the day of Gran May's funeral. We sit in silence for most of the time, watching boats fly by, kayakers navigating their wakes, docks bobbing in the distance.

"So," I finally say, "heard you saw her." She shakes the last bit of the snow cone into her mouth then folds the trash up and sets it down. She looks out over the water.

"Yep," she says. I nod.

"I'm sorry," I tell her. There's another long silence, and I struggle with what to say. This is my time to shine as the big sister, but I know I have no idea what she's going through.

"What was she...what was she like?" she asks. She doesn't look at me, just reaches out to tug on a blade of grass in front of her. I think for a minute.

"Honestly?" I ask. She nods. "For a while there, she really was the best mom. When I was young, she was my everything. We'd have girls' nights. She'd do our hair the same, and we'd watch movies. We'd wear matching pajamas, and she'd always let me fall asleep in her bed when my dad was on trips."

She nods slowly.

"But then I got older, and I realized how...broken she really is," I go on. She turns to me. "My dad...he has total control of everything she does, ya know? How she spends money. Who she socializes with. Everything."

I think for a moment, clasping my hands together between my knees.

"When I was a teenager, I promised myself I'd never be like that. Never take orders. Flash forward a few years, and here I am, preparing to do just that."

She raises her eyebrows, and I remember the conversation I had with my mom just last night.

"Er–I mean, I was. But then I found this place. I found you all. And I don't think I want to take orders anymore," I tell her. Her eyes narrow again, and she nods slowly, and I can see a hint of a smile on the corner of her lips.

She chuckles softly.

"What?" I ask.

"I always told myself she was this hideous beast," Haven says. "Gran May didn't have recent pictures of her or anything, so I just had to make her up in my head. What I thought she'd look like now. I always told myself she had warts all over her face. But it turns out, she's beautiful."

I swallow. This is my moment. The moment to let Haven know that someone, some family, *does* choose her.

"I told her to leave," I tell her. Her eyes widen into saucers, and her lips part slightly.

"You did?" she asks. I nod.

"Yeah. I told her to get off my porch." Haven stares at me for a second then bursts into

a fit of laughter.

"Boss move," she says, giving me knuckles. I laugh with her, bumping my fist to hers.

"Do you wanna come back to the house, hang out for a bit?"

She turns to me and gives me another half-smile.

"Yeah," she says. "I'd like that."

21

___

I made a giant bowl of popcorn, and Haven and I are lying on the couch, watching reruns of *The Fresh Prince of Bel Air*, both of us mouthing most of the lines word-for-word. After another hour or two, the coffee table is loaded with snack wrappers and empty soda cans, and we're both lounging back, nursing our snack hangovers.

"So, what's the actual deal with you and Derrick?" she asks me, and I almost choke on a kernel of popcorn. I wasn't ready for that forward of a question.

"I, um…" I freeze. Derrick and I haven't even really talked about it. Although, I feel like, after last night, it was pretty clear how I was feeling.

"You like him, huh?" she asks, popping another piece in her mouth as she watches TV. I smirk.

"Yeah," I tell her. It doesn't feel scary to tell her, for some reason. It feels…safe. "He's pretty great." She looks at me and nods.

"Just be careful, okay?" I cock my head. "He doesn't date much, and if he does, it's not usually for long. He's just...got some issues. Just be straight with him, cool?"

I nod and grab another fistful of popcorn.

"What about you?" I ask her. "Are you dating anyone?"

"There was this guy back at school for a few months, but we haven't talked much since May died. I've been kinda in a weird place, I guess."

I nod.

"Makes sense," I say. "But you like school?"

"Yeah, I do. I'm good at it, ya know? I enjoy studying. I enjoy asking the questions. I just want to get my degree and get back here. Pick up where May left off— or, I guess, wherever you leave off, if you plan to stay."

She says it casually, but I know she's looking for some sort of response. I smile.

"Every day I spend here, it gets harder and harder to remember what I loved so much about my life before Meade Lake."

She turns to me slowly, one of her dark eyebrows lifting up. I go on.

"After last night, I just...don't know what there is for me to go back to, besides a bunch of bullshit. More lies and plastering on fake faces. Taking over a company I have no business running. A life *I* have no real say in." I sigh and look up at her. "I guess what I'm saying is, I think I want to stay here."

She doesn't say anything, but her eyes are big and round.

"But this is your house, too. And I don't want that to change. I know we still have things to learn about each other, but if you want to come back to your house, I will happily find somewhere else to stay in the meantime."

There's a long pause, and I swallow nervously.

"*Our* house," she says. "And I'd like to move back in. But you don't need to move out."

We smile at each other, and I feel this swelling in my heart. Like the missing pieces of my explosion of a life are sorting themselves out. Like all I needed was time here in this magical place to figure out who I actually am.

I WAKE up the next morning with a bag of chips next to me, and Haven is passed out on the other end of the couch with a water bottle still in hand. We stayed up all night talking, telling stories about our upbringing, laughing about first kisses, talking about our friends. I told her about Charlotte and how she is a piece of my soul. Emma, and how I wasn't sure how much longer our "friendship" would last. I told her about the first time I laid eyes on Derrick at the bar.

She told me about her friends in town and how there weren't a ton of kids her age in Meade Lake growing up. Derrick and Ryder and the girls were all a lot older than her, but they always let her tag along whenever Alma and May got together.

As we sit up, hazily squinting in the morning light, we seem to remember at the same time what today is.

"Shit," Haven says, fiddling with her phone to check the time. "I gotta get back to Alma's. I'm supposed to be a hostess." I check the time, too, jumping up to change. Shit. We overslept. By a *lot*.

"Let me go grab a dress, and I'll take you back. I'll help set up and get dressed there. That is, if you think that'll be okay?"

"Sounds good."

I'm back downstairs in a hot second with a strapless sundress and some strappy sandals in hand, and we're on our way back to Alma's.

The place is a madhouse, at least ten cars already in the driveway, despite the fact that the wedding isn't for another few hours. Teddy's kids are running everywhere with Annabelle trailing behind. Luna and Jules are around back, tying the last of the ribbons on the backs of the chairs, and Alma is at the arbor, fastening some floral arrangements to either side of it. Then I see him with a hammer, nailing a stake into the ground on the side of a tent. Muscles pulling tight on his gray t-shirt, he pauses to wipe his brow when he sees me, and his face breaks into a smile.

I sigh to myself as I take in the sight of him, and I can feel myself completely and utterly falling.

Terrifying.

He winks before bending back down to nail in another stake. I say hi to Jules and Luna and grab a handful of ribbon to help. I help Alma set all the place settings out and make sure that the centerpieces are all perfectly placed. On each one sits a photo of Mila and Ryder, and as I get to a few tables, I see that some of them are old. Teenage versions of Mila and Ryder stare back at me, their smiles so genuine, so pure, so elated. Like they knew then that something big was happening for them.

I look across the lawn again at Derrick, smiling in his direction. Like I know something big is happening for us.

Another hour or so passes, and Luna and Jules leave to go get ready. Pretty much everything is done, and as the band is setting up, I realize that everyone else is scattering to get ready, too.

"What you doin'?" I hear him ask, and I smile before I even turn to him.

"Just figuring I should probably go get ready. I have a date tonight. I wanna look good," I say. He grins as he wraps an arm around my waist and pulls me in for a quick kiss. There's no one around, but it doesn't much seem like he'd care if there were. And that feels kind of good.

"I have a date, too. I'm gonna go get ready myself," he says, kissing my cheek and walking away. I head up to the house and look around, making sure everything inside is done, too. I turn down the hall and knock on Haven's door.

"Come in," she says. When I open the door, she's fiddling with the zipper on a short, pale-pink dress. "Oh, hey. Can you give me a hand?"

"Course," I say, walking over and helping her close it up. I look over her shoulder at our reflections in the mirror. To the plain eye, you'd never know we share DNA. Green eyes to brown, pale skin to dark. But now that I've spent time with her, now that she knows about me, and I know about her, I *feel* like her sister. And as we look at ourselves, I feel like I notice the tiniest bit of a resemblance.

"What are you wearing?" she asks. I hold up the dress I brought, and she nods to her bathroom for me to change. I pull the dress on and look at the mirror. I might be wearing a dress, but I'm a hot mess per usual. My head is a little shiny from being outside; my hair is flat to my shoulders. I grab my bag and put on some mascara, but it doesn't seem to do much.

"Do you have any hairspray?" I ask. And then we both pause. She gives me a knowing look and shakes her head slowly. She tugs on one of her perfect curls.

"Don't really need hairspray here," she says. I swallow and nod.

"Right, yeah."

"But I could do something to it, if you want? I actually really like doing hair. And your hair is like Gran May's."

I smile at her and nod.

After a few minutes, she has twisted and pulled my hair up into a perfect updo that looks fit for a bride—or at least a wedding guest.

"You look great," she says. I stand up and tug my dress into place a bit.

"So do you," I say. As we stare at each other for a minute, she steps toward me and, much to my surprise, wraps her arms around me. I let out a gasp as I hug her back.

"I'm so glad you're what she always hoped you'd be," she says. When she steps back, I see there's a tear in her eye, and I can feel them welling in my own, too. "I'll see you out there."

I walk out of her room, tugging my sandals on as I go, when I hear someone whistle.

"Hot *damn,*" Derrick says, and it makes me jump. "I was waiting here for my date, but I think I'd rather take you instead."

I smile and shake my head as I walk toward him, and he slinks a hand around the back of my neck as he kisses me. He steps back, and I take him in. Derrick in nothing is perfect. Derrick in a suit is a pretty close second.

"I think that can be arranged," I whisper, biting my lip. He offers me his arm and a sly smile, and we walk out the back door. Guests have started to arrive, and Derrick is saying hi and introducing me to people as we walk past. I'm sure I've met most of them, and I'm trying desperately to put names with faces as we walk by. I can see them eyeing us; I can see their wondering eyes as he leads me by hand to the front row. The seats around us continue to fill up until, finally, the band starts to play the "Wedding March." Derrick leans in to me to whisper.

"That's my cue," he says then stands up and walks to the front. He stands on the right side of the arbor and winks at me one more time. As the music plays, Luna makes her way down the aisle, followed by Jules. Teddy and one other groomsman line up behind Derrick, and Alma takes the seat next to me. Haven stands at the head of the aisle, handing out programs.

And then, at the top of the aisle stands Annabelle in a bright-pink dress, her chestnut hair braided into an adorable bun. In one hand, she carries a single lily. The other holds Ryder's hand.

"Let's go, Daddy," she says, and the crowd gives off a collective "aww" as they start to make their way. Ryder clutches her hand tightly as she leads him down, but his eyes never falter from the arbor. When they get to the end of the aisle, Derrick reaches out to grab Ryder's arm and leads him to his spot. He whispers something in his ear, and they both laugh. Ryder kneels down to kiss Annabelle, and she scurries off to take a seat with Haven and Alma and Mila's mother.

Then the music plays again, and Mila appears at the top of the aisle on her father's arm. Her dress is simple and flowy, hugging the curves of her body. Her brown locks lay in casual waves off her shoulders, and though I've been to some very expensive black-tie weddings, she's the most beautiful bride I've ever seen. I look at Ryder, and I know he can't see her from the distance. But I know he can feel how beautiful she is. And as she gets closer, he wipes a single tear from his cheek.

AFTER THE CEREMONY, people scatter throughout the tables, on the lawn, on the dock, laughing, talking, and drinking. Mila's mother takes Annabelle home, and Camille takes her and Teddy's kids home. The dancing starts on the patio when it gets dark, and as I'm listening to Lou talk about the bar, I feel a tap on my shoulder.

"The dance floor is open," Derrick tells me as he spins me toward him. "Uh-uh, sir," Luna calls. "You still owe me a dance from Ryder's *first* wedding." Everyone starts to laugh, including myself, as I playfully step back and let her drag him to the floor. He smiles at me as he walks away.

"I'll be back," he says. "Don't go anywhere."

We watch as the two of them throw each other around, laughing and making jokes as they do. I love the bond that Derrick and the people here all seem to have. Like they've all seen the same peril, the same tragedy, the same absolute bliss from time to time. I yearn for it.

"My boy's got some moves," Alma says, taking a seat next to me. Her hair is twisted back into a low bun, and she's got on a pale-purple dress that she smooths out as she sits. I nod and smile.

"I can see that," I tell her, my eyes never leaving him.

"So," she says, "have you given any more thought about what you want to do?" I turn to her.

"About the money?" I ask. She nods.

"The money," she says, "and my boy." My eyes grow wide, and my lips part. She smiles. "Calm down, baby. Not trying to put you on the spot. But as a mama bear, I just want to get something off my chest."

I swallow.

"Okay," I tell her.

"My boys had it rough as kids, baby. We all did. Their daddy was not a kind man, and he hurt us pretty bad."

I feel my heart rate accelerate—that same helpless feeling I had in the store when I knew something was coming that I couldn't stop. That I couldn't do a damn thing about.

"Those boys watched him put his hands on me over and over again," she says, the calm expression on her face never wavering. "But I was desperate to keep the home together. The family, ya know? Alan brought in most of the money, and I still hadn't gotten my nursing degree. He told me it was a waste of time.

"But one night, he came home drunk—more drunk than usual. He didn't like what I'd made for dinner. I could feel it comin' on, ya know? I always could because of the way the air between us got colder. I told the boys to go into the other room, and they did. But little Derrick…he knew something was coming. He could see it. I'll never forget that look he had in his eyes when Teddy dragged him out of the room. He was only nine.

"I tried to do my best to de-escalate. But it was no use. And when he pulled his belt from his pants, I knew it was going to start. I tried to run, but he caught me.

And when I screamed, the boys stayed where they were, just like I had taught them to. I was lying on the ground, bleeding from the belt, when I saw Alan take the mirror off the wall in front of us. As he lifted it over his head, my baby stepped in front of me. He begged his daddy not to do it. Not to hurt me. But in the midst of his anger, he still brought that mirror down. Only it didn't hit me. It hit Derrick."

I gasp, covering my mouth. I feel tears prickling in my eyes. I look out at the dance floor, his face still lit up as he swings Luna, and now Jules, around, laughing wildly.

"Oh, God," I whisper.

"Thirty-four stitches in his chest," she goes on, and I stare at him, picturing the scar on

his chest that my fingers traced just two nights before. I want to kiss it again, heal it, heal whatever's hurting inside of him.

"So what happened?" I ask. She shakes her head.

"When I took him to the hospital, May was volunteering at the welcome desk. She visited us, brought us gifts and snacks. And afterward, we stayed in touch. She helped us come up with a plan to leave, and that's just what we did. We got a restraining order against him, but to be honest, we didn't need it. Alan never quite forgave himself for what he did to Derrick. It didn't take much to get him to leave. But that's still a parent. That's still their daddy. And when he left, he never contacted us again."

I swallow, staring down at my hands.

"I'm not telling you this for a pity party, honey. I just want to explain to you why my son is so particular about things like, well, love."

My eyes widen as I turn back to her.

"I know it's early," she says, "but there's something different about him with you. He's...hopeful. Like he sees something further than just a few dates. I know I shouldn't even be talking to you about this. I know it's not my place. He's a grown man. But he was my protector, that one. Teddy learned it was safe to love someone. He knew he'd never turn into his dad. Derrick never quite got there. Just be careful with him, baby. And if it ain't right, please let him down easy."

She pats my hand as she stands, kneeling down to kiss the top of my head.

It's right, Alma.

He walks over to me soon after she stands up and sticks out his hand.

"Now," he says, "can I finally have a dance with my date?" I smile and slip my hand into his, letting him pull me to the back corner of the floor. Mila and Ryder are in the center, a handful of people dancing around them, holding their phones into the air to light it up. But when Derrick pulls me into his chest, looping my arms around his neck, I don't see them. I don't hear the music. I just feel him.

"I'm so glad you found me," I whisper after a moment, and he looks down at me. He strokes my cheek and bends down for a kiss. Our foreheads press together, and then his eyes open slowly.

"Come back to my place tonight," he says. My eyes flick up to his, but he won't make contact with me, like he's nervous for my reply.

"Of course," I whisper back. He smiles and kisses the inside of my hand.

"Let's go," he says. He leads me off the dance floor

and starts to say his goodbyes. Other people are leaving around us, so it seems like a good time to slip out.

"I'm gonna go say bye to Mama," he says. "I'll be right back."

I grab my purse off the back of the chair and look around to make sure I'm not missing anything.

"Hey, lady!" I hear Mila call as she comes up from behind me.

"Hey, Mrs. Casey!" I say to her, wrapping her in a hug.

"Thank you for all your help setting up today," she says. "You plan these things for a freakin' year, and go figure, you're *still* not ready day-of." I smile and nod. I know the Meade Lake crew is only a few years older than me, but it seems like our life plans are spaced out by decades. Or, at least, it used to. Before I came here.

Before Derrick.

"Where you off to?" she asks me. I swallow, not prepared to lie.

"I, uh, I think we're going to Derrick's," I tell her. I'm under the assumption that most people here know that *something* is going on between us. They don't know that part of that something was him screwing me on the balcony the other night, but they know that *something* is going on.

Mila's eyebrows shoot up.

"Whoa," she says.

"'Whoa', what?" Jules says, coming up next to us.

"She's going back to Derrick's," Mila says. Jules's eyebrows shoot up.

"What?" I ask.

"He's just never brought a girl back to his place," Jules says. "Even when we were younger. Never brought anyone home to meet Alma. He's very private, and he keeps his family and his home sacred."

I swallow.

"Don't mess it up," Mila says with a playful wink as she leans in for another hug.

And if it's not right, please let him down easy.

22

Derrick opens the door for me and helps me up into his truck. Despite the fact that I was with him the other night, and the other morning, and was very, *very* naked, I'm nervous. My hands are clammy as I digest all the information that's been thrown at me over the last two hours.

He knew he'd never turn into his dad. Derrick never quite got there.

He keeps his family and his home sacred.

"That was a great night," he says, and he pulls the truck onto the road.

"It was," I say, lying back against the headrest and trying to relax. "They looked so happy." He smiles.

"They are."

We turn onto Lakeside Highway and drive a few miles. We pass the store on the right, then after a little while longer, he makes another turn, and I realize we're headed up the mountain. When we get to the top, he turns right, and we drive down a dark, wooded road.

Finally, he turns into a gravel driveway, and at the head of it sits a modest, wood-sided house.

"Well," he says, "this is home." He draws in a long breath, and if I'm not mistaken, he seems nervous, too. He walks around the side of the truck to get me, and I follow him up a paved stone path.

"This is really nice," I tell him, and I mean it. It's homey; it feels safe.

"It's not May's house," he says with a chuckle as he unlocks the front door, "and it's certainly no Georgia mansion." I swallow. He's mentioned Georgia to me only a few times, and each time, it's a reminder that this new version of me—this Kaylee 2.0—is still in its infancy.

"It's perfect," I tell him. The house is much smaller than May's, but it's got plenty of room for one person. Or maybe two. Everything is spotless, not a dish in the sink, not a pillow out of place on the couch.

"Can I get you anything?" he asks, dropping his keys on the kitchen counter and pulling down two glasses from the cupboard above.

"Water is fine," I tell him. "I had a few glasses of wine tonight, and I'm still feeling them." He laughs as he grabs a pitcher from the fridge and pours two big glasses. We gulp it down as we stare at each other from across the kitchen.

"Saw you talkin' to Mama tonight," he says as he sets his empty glass down on the counter. I nod.

"Yeah. I talked to Mila and Jules some, too." He leans back against the counter, gripping it.

"What'd they have to say?"

I suck down the last drop of water and put my own glass down.

"They told me you've never brought a girl up here," I say matter-of-factly. He narrows his

eyes at me as he shifts on his feet.

"They're right."

"What's different this time?"

He bites his lip, like he's not sure if he wants to respond.

"I'M NOT SURE YET," he says. I lean back on my hip and cross my arms over my chest.

"Is this one of those 'you're not like other girls' things?" I ask with a playful grin. Only, I'm not all the way kidding. He shakes his head.

"Nah," he says. "It's one of those 'this feels real' things. And to be honest, I don't think I was ready for that."

I swallow, still staring into those big, beautiful, brown eyes.

"Me either," I whisper.

"I'm assuming Mama gave you the background," he says. I nod. "When I think about my

dad, know what I remember?"

"What?"

"When he'd bring us home water guns."

I tilt my head, and a sad grin spreads across his lips.

"All those times he drew blood from my mama, and then from me, and all I can think

about are the damn toys he brought us. We'd play for hours, and he'd always win, even when it was two against one. I think that's what was so dangerous about him. He seemed happy. Owned his own business at one point. Loved my mom. He seemed like he had it all together. Until he didn't."

"Derrick," I whisper, walking across the floor and standing directly in front of him. He lifts his eyes to me slowly. "Let me tell you something."

I take his face in my hands.

"I am not the only one who will never turn into their parent," I whisper. His eyes drop back to the ground. I slide a hand down to his chest, right over his scar. "You're too good, too beautiful, to ever be like that."

He lets out a sigh then snakes his hands around my waist, pulling me into him. Our lips crash together as I grab hold of his head, keeping him tight to me. He swings me around so that my back is to the counter and lifts me up on top of it. He slides a hand up my leg and under my dress, letting it trail across my panties. The sensation of his fingers on me and the cool granite beneath me sends chills rippling across my skin.

"Cold?" he asks. I nod.

"A little." He tugs me toward him and lifts me off the counter.

"I can fix that," he whispers. He carries me down the hall to the last door and kicks it open as he kisses me, our tongues dancing around each other like it's been years since they've touched. He carries me through his bedroom and into his bathroom, reaching down to turn the water on in the shower. He puts me on my feet and stands back to tug on my dress. It slides down my body, my breasts falling from it as he pulls. He stops to take one into his mouth, and I lean back against the wall for support. He twists the other nipple in his fingers gently then takes the dress the rest of the way off, looping his fingers into the sides of my panties and letting them drop on the floor. I reach out to unbutton his dress shirt and tug it from the top of his pants. He helps me get his pants off, and we kick them to the side.

He steps into the hot water and holds a hand out to me, tugging me in and pushing me up against the cool tiles. He hikes me up, wrapping my legs around him. His hands scour my body while he kisses me, like he wants to feel every inch of me. And I don't mind one bit. I clench my legs around him, feeling what the collision of our bodies has done to him. He drops his head to mine as I rub myself against his length.

"What have you done to me, girl?" he asks. I smile as I gently bite his bottom lip, letting it slide between my teeth.

"Nothing compared to what I want to do," I say. With that, he parts us slightly and goes to reach out of the shower, but I stop him.

"I'm on the pill," I tell him, and his eyes widen.

"You sure?" he whispers. I bite my lip as I look down at our bodies pressed together, his

dark skin on mine, the most beautiful contrast I've ever seen.

"I'm sure," I tell him, pulling him back to me so I can kiss his perfectly round lips again. He pulls back again, this time so that he can slide into me, and I let out a yelp of pleasure as he buries himself inside of me.

"Fuck, Derrick, yes," I moan, the hot water pounding against our skin and the sensation of no barrier making me lose my mind. I clench every muscle around him, never wanting to let go. Never wanting there to be space between us again. I want to hold onto him until we become one, knowing that no one has ever

—or will ever—know me the way he does. Including the people who have known me my entire life.

When we finish, we wash up and get out. He gives me a t-shirt of his to wear, and he pulls down the covers on his bed and holds a hand out.

"Stay?" he asks, and his big brown eyes are pleading. I walk to him and kiss him gently, then flop down on the bed and curl up into a ball on his pillow. He looks down at me, a conflicting look on his face. I pop up.

"Oh, sorry. Is this your side?" I ask. He smiles and shakes his head.

"Nah," he says. "It's yours now."

23

___

He wakes me up with tiny kisses across my bare shoulders, and I decide I never want to wake up any other way. I roll over to him, his head resting on his hand.

"You're the only other person who has ever slept in this bed," he tells me. I run a hand through my hair, suddenly feeling vulnerable in my first-thing-in-the-morning state.

"Well, I'm honored," I tell him, and I'm also a little relieved. I'm not naive enough to not know that a guy that looks like Derrick is definitely *not* a virgin. Especially a guy who's a few years my senior. But there's something special about knowing he's never made love to anyone else in this bed. In this whole house.

There's something special in knowing he's never trusted someone enough to bring them here.

"I have to work at the shop today," he says, "but I want to see you later."

Oh yeah, real life. Forgot about that.

I like how direct he is.

"Oh, yeah," I say. "We should talk about the shop." I slip out of bed and look around for my dress.

"What about it?" he asks, slipping off the other side and pulling his boxers on.

"Well, I know you and May had some plans for it," I say. "I'm meeting with Jeffrey and May's accountant next week to figure out where she left off."

He turns to me slowly.

"So, you mean…"

I smile.

"Yeah. You and Ryder are going to get that expansion," I say. He chuckles and paces toward me so we're just inches apart.

"I don't give a damn about the expansion," he says, cupping my face in his hands and locking his fingers behind my head. "I just like that you have plans to stay here."

I swallow as his lips cover mine.

Yeah, I guess I do.

HE TAKES me back to Alma's to get my car, and I head back to the house to take another shower—this time without the demigod of a man—and go through the ledger again to see what questions I might have for the planner. Haven was staying at Alma's again last night before she moved her things back here sometime this week. As I sit at the kitchen island and flip through the giant book, I notice a pile of mail next to me that Haven must have brought in when she was last here.

I swallow, looking at the top few items all addressed to May. I flip through them—magazines and catalogs, a few letters from banks and doctors' offices who must not have gotten the message that she'd passed. I sigh as I push them to the side. It's strange being here in her wake, like I'm chasing some sort of ghost. Just as I'm turning back to the ledger, I notice one more envelope. But it doesn't have May's name on it; it has mine.

I recognize the perfect script handwriting imme-diately.

It's my mother's.

I swallow as I slip my finger in and tear it open. My hand trembles as I unfold the page,

the same stationery she's had for years, her initials inscribed at the top in gold.

DEAR KAYLEE,

I KNOW this is an unconventional means of communicating nowa-days, but I didn't think that, after our last meeting, you'd be too inclined to take my calls. I know our last meeting wasn't what either of us wanted. I think we're both hurting, Kaylee, and I think time can heal that hurt if we let it.

I'M WRITING to tell you that we need you, Kaylee. The business is in bad shape. We've laid off almost two-hundred more employees over the last month, and there are more coming. Without the women-owned status, we're missing out on a lot of benefits. We can get more federal help. We can save the company and all those jobs.

. . .

I KNOW YOU'RE ANGRY, Kay. I know you're mad at me, and you have questions. Questions I may never be able to answer for you. But this is bigger than us. This is bigger than me and your dad. This affects working people who need this company to survive in order to feed their families. This affects people like Margaret and Tom. And Franklin.

I'M ATTACHING the company's financials so you can see this is no exaggeration. We are losing money by the second, and there's really no other way out of this.

WE NEED YOU, Kaylee. And so do they. We choose family, always.

COME HOME.

LOVE ALWAYS,
  Mom

I CAN FEEL my heart beating louder, harder, until it reverberates through my throat and stomach. I reread her words, and all I can see is the plain manipulation that I was never aware I was a victim of until I got to Meade Lake. The way she and my father use guilt, the way they remind me of what they've given me, of what they've given others. And how they so easily put all that weight back on me.

I swallow back tears—or at least, I try to.

But I can't. Because twenty-three years of lies come spilling out all over the stupid stationery. And all I can see is Franklin. All I can hear are his words in the elevator.

"Is this what you want, Kaylee?"

He knew as much as I did that it wasn't. He wanted the best for me. Always did.

We choose family, always.

I wipe the last of my tears and reach for my phone on the counter.

"Hello?" Jeffrey answers. After our initial meeting, he had given me his personal number. *"Family of May's is family of mine."*

"Jeffrey, hi, it's Kaylee," I say.

"Hey, hon," he answers, but even his sing-song voice isn't enough to lift my mood. "What can I do for you?"

"Is it possible to schedule a meeting with the financial planner today?" I ask.

"To-today?" he asks.

"I know it's short notice," I say. "It's, um, kind of urgent."

"Uh, okay, sure. Let me make some calls. Why don't you come into my office around two?"

"I'll be there," I say.

24

I trudge up the steps of May's house after my meeting with Jeffrey and May's financial planner—who just so happened to be Jules's dad, Tony.

"Are you sure this is what you want to do?" Jeffrey had asked me. I nodded and reluctantly signed the paperwork before Tony whisked it off the desk.

I drop my keys on the front table and kick my shoes off in the foyer. I pad across the hardwood but jump when I see Haven standing in the kitchen, perfectly still.

"Hey," I say, my voice heavy, like I'm carrying the weight of an entire multi-million-dollar company on my back. I walk to the fridge and pull out a bottle of water.

She doesn't respond, so I turn to her, and then I freeze when I see that she's holding the letter from my mother—*our* mother—in her hand. The one I so stupidly left sitting on the counter when I left for Jeffrey's.

"Oh, that…"

"Are you going back?" she cuts me off. I swallow and set my water bottle down on the counter.

"I...I haven't quite worked out—" I start to say, but she holds a hand up.

"Yes or no," she says. "It's a simple question." I stare at her for a moment, her eyes narrowed in on mine.

"Yes," I mutter quietly. "But—"

"Going back where?"

Derrick's voice is quiet, but it booms through the open house. I close my eyes.

This can't be happening.

Haven doesn't take her eyes off of me.

"To Georgia. Mommy Dearest sent a letter," she says, waving it in the air. "Looks like they need my sister here to run back and run their company." I feel the air grow cold and stiff, like I'm being blocked out of something. Derrick stares at me from the doorway, like he's not even sure if he should come farther into the house.

"Kaylee," he whispers, the disappointment palpable in his eyes, in the heavy way his whole body seems to be pulled toward the floor. Like he's already given up.

"They are going to have to lay off hundreds of people if I don't do something," I say quietly. Derrick lifts a hand up and swipes his face.

"Aw, Kaylee," he whispers. "They sunk their teeth into you." He drops his head and

shakes it before he turns to walk back out the door. Before I can say anything else, Haven takes a few steps toward the front door but stops when we are shoulder to shoulder.

"I'll be okay when you go," she says. "I've been left before. But him? I don't know if I can say the same. And you and I both know he deserves so much better."

She follows him out the front door, and I'm left with nothing but my mother's letter, a destroyer of worlds.

. . .

I SPEND the rest of the day calling Derrick, stopping by his house and the store, but to no avail. He's avoiding me, and he knows all the best hiding spots in this place, not me.

I spend the other half of the day calling Haven, but I can't seem to get through to her, either. I toy with the idea of stopping by Alma's but decide that's probably not in anyone's best interest right now. They need their space.

I go back to May's and pack up a bag. As I pull a few shirts from the top drawer, I see the turquoise bracelet I bought to match Haven's. I clasp it around my wrist and hold it close to my chest. Then, I go downstairs, lock the front door, and get in my BMW.

TEN-PLUS HOURS LATER, I'm pulling up in front of Jennings Technology. The parking lot is largely empty now, and as much as I've dreaded coming here, I'm dying to get out and stretch my legs. I could have dressed in office attire, but I decided not to. Not for this. I'm making the rules today.

I grab my badge out of my bag and scan into the building. As I take the elevator up to the top floor of the building and walk through the cubicles, most of the desks are empty. People have gone home for the evening, many of whose days might be numbered here.

I freeze when I get to an empty office, the golden name plate on the door making me cringe.

KAYLEE JENNINGS, SALES MANAGER.

I shudder and slide it out of its holder.

As I walk farther down the hall, I see one desk light still on, and I smile. I knew I could count on him to be right where I needed him, right when I needed him to be there. His glasses are slid down toward the tip of his nose, and he's mumbling something to himself as he reads off of his computer screen. The top of his head is peppered with black and white tufts of short cut hair.

"Franklin?" I ask. He jumps a little, spinning around in his chair.

"Kaylee?" he says, standing up to wrap me in a warm hug. "What are you doing here? I'm so happy to see you."

"I'm happy to see you, too," I tell him, trying like hell not to get choked up.

"It's nice to see your face around here," he says. "Word is, these are some uncertain times for the company. I hope your daddy is okay."

His words crush me like an anvil.

Because my daddy sure doesn't give a damn if Franklin is okay or not. My daddy is just worried about his fortune. His status as Georgia's leading man. His *power*.

"Do you mind coming with me to his office for a moment?" I ask him. He cocks his head to one side, and I can tell he's uncertain. "It shouldn't take long."

I see him swallow, and I realize he thinks this is it. He thinks this is the end for him. I put my hand on his.

"It's gonna be okay, Franklin," I tell him. He nods and follows me down the hallway to my father's office. I don't knock; I just push the cracked door open.

He looks disheveled, his shirt wrinkled, his normally perfectly styled hair out of place. Like he knows this is the end for him. When he sees me, his jaw drops.

"Kaylee," he says, pushing to stand. He walks toward me, arms outstretched, but freezes when he sees Franklin in the doorway behind me.

"Franklin, can you give us a moment?" he asks.

"I asked him to come," I say. "We need to talk." He swallows and nods, leading us to the table in the corner of his insanely huge office. On the back wall is a poster-size print of the three of us when I was in middle school. It was taken at our beach house for a local magazine feature on my dad and the company. He carried issues of the magazine around with him for months.

We sit down, and I reach into my bag and pull out the folder of paperwork that Jeffrey and Tony had prepared for me. Then I pull out my laptop.

"I got Mom's letter," I tell him. I can tell my father is out of sorts. Not being in the know is completely out of the ordinary for him. And being in control is completely out of the ordinary for me. At least, it used to be. I look right at him, Derrick's words ringing in my ears.

They sunk their teeth into you.

"I read through the company's financials and had my accountant do the same," I say. My dad pulls on his suit jacket and shifts in his chair. Franklin does the same.

"I'm not coming back to work. I'm not taking the Sales Manager position."

My father pushes forward in his chair, and I can see the vein in his forehead starting to pop out. He's feeling the reins being pulled straight from his hands. But I go on before he can protest.

"But I will help get this company back on its feet— under a few conditions."

He leans back in his chair, his eyebrows knitted together.

"I looked through the files Mom sent and took the liberty of logging into the system to do some investigating of my own. Are you aware that out of two thousand employees, only a little less than six percent of your employees are minority?"

My father blinks.

"And that out of thirty-five executives, not a single one of them is a person of color?"

He blinks again, and Franklin clears his throat.

"That brings me to my recommendation. Under minority-owned business status, the company can qualify for state and federal help and be given priority contract work, bringing in more revenue."

He blinks faster now, then his eyes dart from me, to Franklin, back to me.

"Minority-owned?" he asks. I nod.

"Yes." I open my laptop and press a button to start a video call. In a moment's time, Jeffrey and Tony both appear on my screen. "This is Tony Prince, my financial advisor. And this is Jeffrey Tate, my lawyer."

My dad's eyes grow wide as he looks at the men, then to me.

"Your lawyer?"

I nod.

"I've had Jeffrey here draw up some paperwork that I have for you. In it, it explains that you will be stepping down as CEO and signing ownership of the company over to Franklin J. Sommers in order to apply for and obtain minority-owned business status," I say. Jeffrey smiles and holds up the packet of paperwork he wrote up for me as I simultaneously slide the copy for my father across the table. Franklin stares at me, his jaw to the floor.

My father is completely speechless, his face red and splotchy, his eyes darting back and forth across the paperwork. He thinks for a minute then slides it across the table to me forcefully.

"You think you're just gonna walk in here after all this time and take *my* company away?" he asks through gritted teeth. "I built this company from the ground up. That's *my* name on this building." I know that if he didn't have an audience, his cool would have been completely lost by now. But I keep mine. Easy and steady.

"That's true," I say. "You did start the company. But if memory serves, you had a partner originally, who happens to be your longest standing employee. Mr. Franklin J. Sommers."

My father's eyes slowly move across the table to Franklin, who is just staring down at the paperwork.

"That doesn't solve the fact that we're running out of money as we speak. I still can't afford to pay everyone, and getting minority status will take months, if not longer," my father says, running a hand through his over-gelled hair.

"That's where I come in," I say. "I recently came into an inheritance."

My father's eyes dart back to me, one eyebrow raised.

"Tony?" I say. Tony clears his throat.

"Ah, yes. After running some numbers based on the financials your wife sent, we determined the total amount you'd need for overhead to keep the company afloat for the next six months," he says. "You'll see that on page three. Now, we also determined that while there have been layoffs and salary freezes, all thirty-five of the executives have received not only their annual raises, but also their bonuses. Is that correct?"

My dad looks at Franklin sheepishly then wets his lips.

"Yes," he mutters.

"If every executive forfeits their raises and bonuses and agrees to take a salary reduction of just three percent over the next fiscal year, you can save upwards of fifty positions."

"And what about the rest?"

"I can cover those salaries with a one-time payment that will provide enough overhead for the next six months. All you need to do is sign this."

I slide another packet of paper toward him, and Jeffrey pipes up.

"What you see here, Mr. Jennings, is the change of ownership agreement. You'll want to have your lawyers look this over and sign that so we can get the ball rolling on making Mr. Sommers the owner. The next page is the diversity agreement."

"What the hell is that?" my father asks.

"It's a fair hire clause. It says that, moving forward, Jennings Technology will make a conscious effort to diversify its workforce. Oh, and there's one more thing. Kaylee?"

I clear my throat.

"Under this agreement, I would be a partner of the company. Any return on investment will go back into salary increases for everyone *except* the executives. As CEO, Franklin will also appoint a Diversity Oversight Committee to ensure that the agreement is followed through."

There's a long pause, and I hang up with Jeffrey and Tony.

Finally, my father looks up to me.

"Franklin, can you excuse us?" he says. Franklin nods and stands slowly. Our eyes meet, and I can see there's so much he wants to say, but he doesn't need to. He closes the door behind him, and I turn back to my dad.

"What if I refuse?" he asks. I sigh and bend down to put my things back in my bag. My time here is almost done.

"Then, when you have to let go hundreds of employees, that's on you," I tell him.

He rubs his temples then folds his hands together in front of him.

"I'll do it," he mutters, and I nod. It's a sweet victory, but one that comes with its own black cloud of truth: this is it for me and my parents. I stand up and walk toward the door.

"You have till the end of the week to have everything signed. Jeffrey's information is in the folder, so you can send that over to him."

I pull the door open and walk out into the hall when he calls my name.

He stands with his hand on the door jamb, looking down at the ground.

"How could you do this?" he asks, his voice shaky. There's so much to say, so much I want to scream. But I'm stilled by an overwhelming sense of calm and clarity. I ignore his question. I ignore one more example of his manipulation. My eyes pierce his.

"Be honest with me, Dad. Did you make Mom give

her up because she wasn't yours, or did you make her give her up because she was black?"

My question leaves him completely dumbfounded. Completely shattered. He's a shell of the man I once knew and loved. The man I thought could rule the world. Turns out, he's just a man who trampled on a lot of other people to get where he is. When I realize he has no answer, I turn to walk out of the office.

"We choose *family*."

I look up to him, our eyes meeting one last time.

"That's exactly what I'm doing."

I round the corner to where Franklin sits, but his desk is empty. When I walk out to the elevators, he's there, waiting. He smiles as he presses the button.

"I thought we could take one last elevator ride together," he says, holding the door open for me.

We're quiet as we ride down, and I think of all the early-morning conversations we've had here.

"That was...that was a really amazing thing you just did, Kaylee," he says just as the car is pulling to a stop on the ground floor. He turns to me. "You just changed a lot of people's lives. Including mine."

He pulls me in for a long hug, and I squeeze him tight.

"You're going to do amazing things," I tell him.

"You already are," he tells me before turning toward the doors. As I walk across the lot and pull my keys from my bag, I'm reliving the last few moments. The sheer terror on my father's face, the gratefulness on Franklin's.

"Kaylee." My mother's voice rattles me from my thoughts just as I point my key fob toward my car.

"Mom," I say. "How did you know I was here?"

She shrugs.

"I didn't. Supposed to be meeting your father down here to go to dinner," she says. There's a pause. "So this is what we've become, huh? Mother and daughter who don't even know when the other is in town?"

I look down at the ground.

"You made your choice, Mom. And I won't make the same one."

"Wait," she says, putting her hand on mine before I open the car door. I look at her hand on mine, then back up to her, my eyes carrying a warning in them. She peels her hand back slowly, like she's afraid.

"Tell me one last thing," I say. Her eyes are wide and pleading. "Is her father Billy?"

My mother closes her eyes, tears streaming out of the sides of them. She nods.

"How can I find him?"

She sniffles and reaches into her purse to grab a pen and an old envelope. She writes down a phone number and hands it to me.

"What is this?"

"His phone number," she says. I look at her.

"You still know it by heart?" I ask. She nods. I fold the piece of paper up and tuck it into my bag. Our eyes meet again before I slip into my car and turn on the ignition. I pull out of the spot, out of the parking lot, and onto the main road.

My mother fades away in my rearview mirror, along with every trace of the life that was once all I knew.

25

It's a little past twelve noon when I finally make my way back over Meade Bridge, and seeing the water beneath me breathes life back into me that I so desperately need. A full day of driving combined with a last, life-altering encounter with my parents has left me feeling like a shell, but I don't have time to sit around. I have shit to fix.

I asked Jeffrey to call the meeting at his office, and he did just as I asked. I pull into the parking lot at the firm and head inside. Tara is at the front desk, perfect smile on her face.

"Morning, Kaylee," she says. "They're all back there."

I nod.

"All of them?"

She smiles.

"Yes. Your sister is there. Derrick's there, too," she says.

I turn to the conference room at the end of the hall, take a breath, and push the door open.

Around the table, every business owner that May ever made deals with, or planned to, sits. They're chatting, probably wondering why it is Jeffrey called them here today. Probably wondering what the fate of their endeavors is going to be. When eyes start to land on me, a collective hush falls over the crowd. I clear my throat and stand at the front of the room.

"Morning, everyone. Thanks for all coming in on such short notice."

My eyes meet Derrick's, and they're wide and full of question. He and Haven sit at the back of the room together.

"I know there have been some questions, since the death of my grandmother, on the status of loans and projects. I just wanted to let you all know that all loans will still be processed, and any projects slated for this year will continue as planned."

A few people whisper *yes* to themselves; a few actually clap.

"Thank you so much," one woman says.

"This is such a relief," another man says.

"Jeffrey will be working on the agreements for everything," I tell them, "but expect to get back to where we were within a month's time. I also wanted to note that I'll be moving to the area permanently. I'll be at May's house, so feel free to stop by anytime."

I look at Haven.

"That is, if my roommate will still have me."

She smiles at me from the back of the room, a twinkle in her eye.

"She'll still have you," she says. I smile and nod in her direction.

They all stand and shake my hand as they leave,

grabbing paperwork from Jeffrey and making appointments with Tara at the door. I take a deep breath and walk toward the front door just as someone grabs my hand. When I whip around, I see it's Ryder.

"You don't know how happy this makes us," he says, pulling me in for a hug. Mila wraps her arm around my neck and joins in.

"We're so happy you're sticking around," she says. "We'll see you real soon."

I walk down the hall, but I don't see him anywhere. I walk out into the parking lot and see him leaning up against his truck. When I walk by, he pops off. I stop in my tracks, directly in front of him.

"You came back," he says just above a whisper. I nod.

"You were the one who told me I wouldn't become my parents. I had to prove that to myself," I say with a shrug. "But I'm back now. For good. I was never leaving here. I was never leaving *you.*"

He takes a few steps toward me, slowly at first then faster. He stops just inches in front of me.

"What have you done to me, girl?" he whispers then bends down, letting his lips crash into mine, scooping me off the ground.

"I think that's him!" I say, shaking Derrick's arm from the backseat. I look at my sister in the passenger seat, staring out of the windshield. She's clutching onto the bracelet I gave her, spinning it around nervously.

A white car pulls up in the lot across from us and parks. We're in the lot of a recreational park in Virginia where we agreed to meet, and we got here early. We've been keeping busy by stuffing ourselves with snacks and playing I Spy, but now, the time has come.

The man gets out of the car and closes his door, and we follow suit. Haven gets out slowly, clutching onto the door handle for dear life. I stand next to her and take her hand. We walk to the middle of the parking lot, and we can make out his face.

He's got some wrinkles around his eyes, but they point to light-brown, speckled irises—sort of like Haven's.

He has smooth, round lips, just like my sister's. And dark skin, like my sister's.

"Billy?" I ask as we get closer. He nods.

"That's me," he says. I look at Haven, and her chest heaves up and down as she stares at him.

"You must be Haven," he says, his voice trembling. She nods slowly. "I've been waiting your whole life to meet you. I just didn't know it until right now."

With that, she lunges forward, wrapping her arms around him. Derrick takes my hand as we all fight back tears.

Billy squeezes her tight, and they sway together for a moment. "I'm sorry I've missed so much," he says. "If I had known, I wouldn't have missed a second. But I'm here now, and I'd really like to not miss much more."

ONE YEAR LATER

"This is the only place in town still open today, I think," he says as he reaches through the window of the snow cone shop and grabs two for us. I kick my sandals off and hook my fingers through them then take my cone from him and plop down in the grass.

"Don't spill on your dress," he says, eyeing my wedding gown as he tugs on his tie to loosen it. I smile.

"I only plan to wear this sucker once," I say, nodding toward it, "so a little color won't hurt."

He smiles and leans forward, our snow-cone-chilled lips touching.

"You look beautiful, Mrs. Thomas," he says just before stealing a bite off the top of my cone.

"Hey! Watch yourself, Mr. Thomas. When I said, 'what's mine is yours,' I did *not* mean my snow cones."

He laughs and kisses the tip of my nose. We snuck out of our own reception to get a breather. We look out over the water, snuggled up against each other, my hair slowly sliding out of the beautiful updo Haven had put it in.

Everything is quiet, peaceful, until he laughs to himself.

"What?" I say, folding up the paper of the cone and setting it down on the ground.

"I just can't believe this is where we are now," he says, looking down at the new shiny ring on his finger. "I can't believe you're mine."

I smile back at him, nestling into the crook of his neck.

"May would have loved that we got married, huh?" I ask. He smiles that same smile that made me fall to my knees a year ago and still does today.

"Yeah," he says. "I won't lie; she loved me. She would definitely approve." I laugh as he pulls me closer, kissing my temple. "I'm sorry your family wasn't here today."

I look up at him and smile.

"They were."

PROLOGUE

"Jules, where do you want this one?" Kaylee asks me as she carries another box in from my car.

"What's in it?" I ask. She shrugs and sets it down. We've been unpacking in my new spot for about three hours now, and Kaylee's the only one who hasn't quit on me. I think it's because she's the new girl of the group, and she wants to stay on my good side. But whatever the reason, I'm taking all the help I can get.

I start digging through it, and it doesn't take long until I realize it's a box of stuff from high school. Yearbooks, movie stubs, concert tickets, and stacks of old photos. Kaylee sits down next to me on the hardwood and grabs a handful of pictures from the box as I start flipping through yearbooks. *Eesh.* No one should have to look at my freshman school photo. No one.

I grab the next book. Sophomore year was a little bit better.

My heart skips a beat when I realize what year that was. The year I met him.

I close the book and hop up, walking to the kitchen island and grabbing another box to see where it needs to go.

"Oh my gosh," Kaylee shrieks. "Is this *Derrick?*"

I walk over to peer down at the awkward photo she has of all of us, the summer after senior year. The summer before everything changed for all of us, the summer that life really took hold. I chuckle as I take the faded photo, stroking the corners as I look down at it. Me, Derrick, Ryder, Luna, and Kirby, all jumping off a dock at the same time.

"Yep," I tell her. "Cute, huh?"

"Oh, gosh, look at Luna here," she says, handing me another. "Was she ever awkward?"

I shake my head.

"Nope. Been a Greek goddess since day one. Does *wonders* to have someone like that as your best friend," I say. Kaylee looks at me and rolls her eyes.

"Oh, stop it. As if you're not gorgeous," she says, then turns back to her photos.

I find a box of towels and start pulling them out, walking them toward the linen closet at the end of the hallway. I'm already loving having my own space, my own organization, my own system for how things should go.

I wasn't always ready to leave my mom's house. In fact, there was a time when I thought I'd *never* be able to. But once I was, I got out of there as fast as I could, and found this little place up on the mountain that's perfect. Close enough to my mom's where I can check in, far enough away for me to feel like I can actually breathe.

"Hey, who's this?" Kaylee asks, holding another photo in my direction.

I walk back to her and take it out of her hands, peering down at it. My eyes widen into big saucers, my pulse picks up its pace beneath my skin.

I remember this day so well, the day after one of Shane's big wins. He'd broken one of the state records in the 200 freestyle, and Tommy and I had painted our whole bodies, almost from head to toe in navy blue paint with Shane's initials on our stomachs.

"That's Tommy," I tell her, running my finger across his perfect grin, that one that's burned into my memory, stamped on my heart. She nods. She's heard about Tommy. She knows I lost him years ago.

"And is this...?" she asks, holding up another photo, one that nearly brings me to my knees. I nod slowly, staring down at the two teenagers in the photo, looking at each other with such loving eyes that I know everyone around us had to suspect something.

He's hoisting me into the air, and I'm holding his face, peering down at him after yet *another* one of his wins. This photo doesn't look like two best friends. It looks like two people who found everything they could ever be looking for in another person.

"Yeah," I say. "That's Shane."

She nods again. She knows I lost him, too.

I lost them both that year, in different ways. Tommy didn't want to leave me. He didn't want to leave us. He had so much more life to live.

But Shane, Shane chose to leave. He decided to live his life. Only, he decided to live it without me.

THE MEADE LAKE SERIES

Did you enjoy Stones Unturned?

Read Back to Shore, Ryder and Mila's story

And

In Winters Past, Jules and Shane's story

Sign up for my newsletter for updates and chances to win free goodies!

ACKNOWLEDGMENTS

This book is so damn special to me, because it's the first book I ever wrote. The bones of this story and these characters are over a decade old, and I am still just as crazy about them as I was back then. HUGE thanks to you, sissy, for always reading, loving, and encouraging me to keep doing this. I think you love my stories more than I do, and that means the world.

To my amazingly supportive tribe of writers and bloggers and readers who are CONSTANTLY supporting me, reading blurbs, looking at covers, and commiserating with me, I adore each and every one of you, and I would be totally lost without you.

Kate, thank you for being my biggest fan. LYLAS. Lilly Pop, as always, I don't know where I'd be without ya. Love you the most. Mom, dad, and Dust, love you always.

To my babies, thanks for being my inspiration day in and day out simply by smiling or laughing, or even screaming for no reason. I love being your mama.

To everyone and anyone who has ever done the right thing even when it was the hard thing, I hope you see yourself in this book. You may not have known it, but you were my inspiration, too.

ABOUT T.D. COLBERT

T.D. Colbert is a romance and women's fiction author. When she's not chasing her kids or hanging with her husband, she's probably under her favorite blanket, either reading a book or writing one. She lives in Maryland, where she was born and raised. For more information, visit www.tdcolbert.com.

Follow T.D. on TikTok, Instagram and Twitter, @taydanaewrites, and on Facebook, Author T.D. Colbert, for information on upcoming books!

Are you a blogger or a reader who wants in on some secret stuff? Sign up for my newsletter, and join **TDC's VIPs** - T.D.'s reader group on Facebook for exclusive information on her next books, early cover reveals, giveaways, and more!

OTHER BOOKS BY T.D. COLBERT:

T.D. Colbert's Author Page

NOTE FROM THE AUTHOR

Dear Reader,

I can't tell you what it means that you've decided, out of all of the books in all the world, to read mine.

If you enjoyed reading it as much as I enjoyed writing it, please consider leaving an Amazon or GoodReads review (or both!). Reviews are crucial to a book's success, and I can't thank you enough for leaving one (or a few!)!

Thank you for taking the time to read *Stones Unturned*.

Always,
  TDC
  www.taylordanaecolbert.com
  @taydanaewrites

Made in United States
Orlando, FL
28 January 2023

29158633R00155